CW00972873

PENNY A LOOK,
TUPPENCE A FEEL

Penny a Look, Tuppence a Feel

Barry Baddock

JANUS PUBLISHING LTD
Cambridge, England

First published in Great Britain 2013
by Janus Publishing Company Ltd,
The Studio
High Green
Great Shelford
Cambridge CB22 5EG

www.januspublishing.co.uk

Copyright © Barry Baddock 2013

British Library Cataloguing-in-Publication Data
A catalogue record for this book is available from the British Library

ISBN 978-1-85756-813-4

All rights reserved. No part of this publication may be
reproduced, stored in a retrieval system or transmitted in any form or
by any means, electric, mechanical, photocopying, recording or
otherwise, without the prior permission of the publisher.

The right of Barry Baddock to be identified as the author
of this work has been asserted by him in accordance with
the Copyright, Designs and Patents Act 1988.

Cover design and illustrations: Robert Page

Printed and bound in the UK by
PublishPoint from KnowledgePoint Limited, Reading

Stories have to be told or they die, and when they die, we can't remember who we are or why we're here.

Sue Monk Kidd, *The Secret Life of Bees.*

Contents

Foreword

One time I stole goosegogs from the back of Mr Bonney's cart. I stuck 'em in me knickers! And just then, I saw the policeman coming and I thought he'd seen me stealing the gooseberries. And I was so frightened that I wetted myself! Then – would you believe it? – when he'd gone, I took them gooseberries home and washed 'em in Dad's water tank. And then I ate 'em! Jean

In the autumn, we used to go acorning – collecting acorns in a bag, to feed the pigs on the estate. The bags were collected every Monday and we'd get one and sixpence for a bushel, ninepence a bushel for horse chestnuts. We used to give some to Aunt Nelly, 'cos Aunt Nelly had a pig. Then, one time, Mum gave Dad all the money we'd earned acorning, so he could to go to the pub. Now that wasn't fair, was it? It was hard work, pulling them bags. Doreen

I used to clean at the Innes house in Manor Lane. It was a big old house, a lovely house. Our sister Mabel worked there too, years before me. But it was ever so eerie. And I had to go back there at night, on my bike, just to turn the bed down! So the corners were just right, like a triangle. But I was quite a little spitfire. I'd rear up at things. One time, Lady Innes said something that I didn't approve of, and I threw the brush at her! Joanie

The boys'd chase us round the lake. And they'd be chanting: 'Penny a look, tuppence a feel. Three to go round the hairy wheel!' Well, Ray Bumpstead, he caught me once. 'Right, Molly, you put your hands in me trouser pockets,' he said, 'you'll feel two ping pong balls – further down,

further down – go on ...!' Well, I met him years later, in
Whiting Street, just like that. And I reminded him about –
you know. He said, 'Ah, they ain't ping pong balls any
more, Molly, they're more like bloody currants!' He died
next week, poor old bugger. Molly

Jean, Doreen, Joanie and Molly are sisters – the last
survivors of eleven children born in a single bedroom in a
Suffolk village between the World Wars.

They love to talk about their growing up, the sisters. And
their stock of memories is amazingly varied: diamonds
mixed with jagged grit; generalities flavoured by beautiful,
sharp-edged vignettes. Their anecdotes portray a life that
has gone: a life shaped by church, school, rectory, pub,
institute and the countryside. They tell of the traffic of
childbirths and funerals, of local characters and simple
pleasures, of drudgery and drunkenness, all-too-common
sickness and loss, bizarre oddities and of a thousand daily
acts of kindness and lending a hand. The four sisters are
among the dwindling few who can still remember that life.

Throughout all of their childhood, British agriculture
was in a state of chronic depression. Farm employment fell
by nearly a third between the World Wars, and the area
under plough by a quarter. The lives of village families were
inevitably formed and coloured by the persistent dire state
of farming. Practically all of them knew hardship and lived
in relative poverty.

Rich as the sisters' memories are, they have tended to shift
and change and, with retelling, to acquire new shapes and
hues. Maddeningly, the women have described an episode in
careful detail one day, then, on the next, embellished it with
fresh characters or a new twist. Sometimes, I have been dazed
by their shameless inventiveness, but have come to accept it
as natural. For we are all but bundles of memories, and in the
widening kaleidoscope of our past, it is inevitable that these
memories become repainted, bent and distorted.

In this collection of tales, I have indulged in inventiveness of my own and have reached beyond the sisters' recollections. More exactly, I have tried to seek out the thoughts, motives, passions and misgivings that drove individuals in that small village in the long-ago. The result is these stories of hidden loves, secret fears and private strivings. Each of them has been bred from the fecund soil of the sisters' authentic memories. The writing of them has given much pleasure: I hope that the reading of them will do so too. Most of all, I wish very much that they will be appreciated by the ladies for whom they were written: Mrs Jean Baddock, Mrs Doreen Duell, Mrs Joan Sansom and Mrs Molly Baldwin.

My thanks to Rob Page for the evocative cover design and for his illustrations. I am grateful, too, to Edward Fenton of Day Books, for his perceptive eye and his comments. And I am indebted to the members of *Write Now!*, the Bury St Edmunds writers' group, led by George Wicker. Honest critics and good friends, they have been the best of companions during my writing endeavour.

Olli

Joanie: *Dad could have been a well-off bloke if he hadn't drunk so much.*

Jean: *Seven shillings a week he gave Mum! He was a wicked man! If there was money in the house, it'd be gone next morning. He'd nick it – for drink!*

Sharp gusts banged against Olli's legs and flung batches of leaves down into his well. Tightening his neck muffler, he pressed on. The first bricking at Blunston's place was finished. So now, at five o'clock on a grey-washed October day, he had come back to the Institute well, to take out the last braces.

Before he started, Olli bent over the well and peered down, to examine the spring water at the bottom. He stared harder. A solid black shape was now obscuring the circular reflection. He peered for another minute, his lips tight. Then

Olli walked back to his cart and hauled out the grappling irons. He eased them down and began to fish up the body.

It was a young man of twenty or twenty-one. Olli had seen him in the village from time to time, but he didn't know the man's name. He was dressed much like Olli himself, in the hard-wearing grey serge trousers and leather belt of a farm labourer. So waterlogged were the man's shirt and waistcoat that Olli could see the outline of his ribs. He noted, too, the incongruity of the bicycle clips still fixed to the bottom of his trousers.

Doreen: *We should never have been poor. But he'd treat people in that pub. 'Good old Olli!' they'd say. He was useless as a husband. He'd spend every night at the pub. He wasn't the worst one in the village. But he was one of the worst.*

Olli was thirty, eight years married, when the war broke out. 'Dad's War', his daughters called it. He took the King's shilling and, in khaki and puttees, left the village to make his amazing journey in God's hands to the edge of the world – to France, a name known only from schoolbook and song.

Molly: *When Dad was away, Mum believed he was having the time of his life with them French mademoiselles. She didn't trust Dad one bit!*

Olli crossed the sea as a soldier, to serve King and Country in the horse artillery. During uneasy hours of truce, it was his task to seek a way through the clouds of cordite smoke, to pick out of the quagmire men who were still alive, and to bear them on stretchers to the Red Cross cart. And whenever the Chief-of-Staff's strategy called for a new battalion to be moved in, it was Olli's duty to clear the trenches of corpses and inter them at a hygienic distance behind the lines.

Doreen: *Dad never did talk about his war, did he?*

Molly: *Well, the only thing I remember him telling me – he was in this trench, looking for survivors, you know. And just when he'd given up, he heard this sound – which he thought was mud slipping in the trench wall, after the rain, you know? Well, he didn't think anything about it. Then, just when he finished stacking up, he saw this arm sticking out, and it was this chap, dead. And, 'course, it had been him moaning. It wasn't the mud at all.*

Twenty-six sons of the parish are named on the marble Roll of Honour at Saint Leonard's Church. Of those who returned, many sought the comfort and sanctuary of The Six Bells rather than the church. Olli didn't drink, though. Not at first, anyway. Instead, he gave himself stoically to the harsh grind that was the well-sinker's life. The village was where he had begun and the village was where he was now, to earn the family's living again. He took up where he had left off, and did not speak of his war.

Molly: *Mum was a moaner. She was real nagger. If Dad was in a good mood, or just came home from work, or whatever, she'd always try to upset him, and to nag him.*

Jean: *He was a real swine, though. He took my paper money once, what I'd earned. I'd just left it lying on the sideboard, and it was gone, just like that. For drink!*

Doreen: *His drinking was a curse – a curse on the whole family.*

Jean: *Too true!*

Doreen: *But he wasn't a bit violent, was he? 'Oh, don't hit them, Maud,' he'd say. And he'd go off to bed, like a little pussycat …*

Joanie: *We used to be thrilled to bits when he went to bed, didn't we?*

Doreen: *Just like a little pussycat. But he squandered his money.*

Olli laid out the dead man beside the well and bent to peer at the pinched, bony face. Clumps of leaves clogged the eye sockets. The mouth and face were smeared with strands of wet grass.

Olli straightened up. He knew his next step was to go and report the business to P.C. Sturgeon, at the police house. So he laid his tools and grappling irons next to the body, and eased himself out through the wooden gate.

Molly: *You know, I think he always regretted not getting to that man in time. So he could see him again after the war, and say to him, 'You know, I saved your life.' But he was too late.*

Carefully closing the gate after him, Olli turned to make his way towards the police house.

Then he heard it.

The sound of a man's groan.

Olli paused as if he had been struck. Then he turned and lurched back towards the gate. At the same moment, a sudden cloud blackened the dim evening light and flung out a squall of rain. Damp leaves smashed into his eyes. He lost his vision for a long moment, and wrestled frantically with the gate. Wrenching it open, he imagined that he heard another moan.

Inside the Institute grounds, he collapsed against the fencing, and slid heavily to earth. Now faces – the faces of all his nightmares – flooded his brain. The faces of torn, suffocated men. Accusing faces, their eyes gaping through blood and filth and mud and spittle. He smelt cordite and lived again his obscene duty of bundling half-living, shattered men onto a cart, as he shut out their agonised screaming.

Then, finally, he saw again the face he had met in the night a thousand times over. And heard again the whimper of the man he had failed. For whom he had been too late.

The rain was thicker now, transforming village soil into the black morass of his nightmares. Gibbering and retching, Olli clambered on his hands and knees across the mud to reach the man beside the well. His shoulders quaking, he straddled the dead body and clutched the cold face to his chest. But he was too late. Too late.

Cursed and broken beneath the grey October sky, Olli wept in Hell and never found his way again.

Patience Frost

Doreen: *Why were we so frightened of Patience Frost? We were frightened, weren't we?*

Jean: *Well, she was round-shouldered and hunched and creepy. She never mixed.*

Molly: *She had walking sticks, didn't she? And we had to pass that cottage of hers when we went to school! All her curtains were drawn, but she used to peer at us through them curtains. All the kids felt the same. Nobody wanted to go near Patience Frost.*

Jean: *She had a husband lost in Dad's War. That's what Mum told me.*

Joanie: *Well, me and Dolly Grainger, we passed her cottage one day …*

Doreen: *She was a brick short of a load, Dolly Grainger.*

Joanie: *Yes, she was a simpleton, wasn't she? Born of a brother and sister. Dolly Grainger was loopy.*

Doreen: *She used to go shouting up the lane.*

Joanie: *Anyway, me and Dolly Grainger, we passed Patience Frost's cottage one time, just when she was drawing water from the well. I didn't see her till the last moment. Well, I was scared stiff! But Dolly Grainger, she walked right up to her and says, 'There's enough blue in that sky to make a sailor's trousers!' She'd heard it at school, you see. She was just showing off, Dolly Grainger, she didn't have any fear of Patience Frost. And you know what the old woman said? She said 'I'll make you a pair, if you like, my dear!' She had a cracked sort of voice, as if she'd got laryngitis or something. Well, it was a sad voice, when I think about it.*

Doreen: *It was. It was sad.*

Joanie: *Well, on our way home, them swallows, all them swallows – they'd built their nests in the eaves of her cottage, you know? They followed us home. They came curving through the air together, right above our heads, singing like beggars. Sweee … ! Oh, it was like music. It was – oh, a lovely sight!*

It is hard to believe that Patience Frost may once have been a pretty woman. But if a flame had ever burned for her, its life was brief. She had married a Guards officer, it was said, but no one seemed to know where the story came from.

In an earlier age, the lonely, bent woman might have hoarded wolfberry and brains of cat, and laid dead frogs on a stone beneath the moon. Indeed, there were some unkind persons who claimed that, when Patience Frost looked in the mirror at night, she saw slit eyes and pointed ears.

But, slanderous village talk apart, little was actually known about her. She was too crippled to go to church. So, patience in name and nature, she seems to have spent her long and cavernous years in the company of her ticking clock, measuring out the rhythms of the seasons.

Sometimes, she would be seen in her garden, watching red fire in the sky and the fleets of crows carping in the high trees. Or listening to the shrill of starlings and blackbirds and the weeping of doves.

Jean: *She used to keep a canary in a cage, which she hung up in a laburnum tree in her garden. I remember that singing bird among the yellow trailers of the laburnum. Used to sing its heart out, it did. I was fascinated by it.*

Tramps knew Patience Frost. If one ever came to her door with a tin can around his neck, she would give him sugar or hot water, so he could make himself some tea. Sometimes one would sing a song for her, and Patience Frost would bring him bread or some soup, beneath the laburnum tree.

Doreen: *Them tramps, they'd be really scruffy. Mrs Dunham hated them. She was Patience Frost's neighbour. Remember Mrs Dunham?*

Molly: *Well, Mum didn't like tramps either, did she? She was always nervous when they came a-begging. And if you didn't give 'em anything, they put a curse on you. That's why Mum always gave 'em something. Or she'd make us all hide under the table, so they wouldn't see us.*

Doreen: *Remember the time Mrs Dunham went round to Patience Frost? To complain about her receiving them tramps? 'Cos Patience Frost was the only one in the village who ever gave them time of day.*

Molly: *Well, they were vagrants, weren't they? They spread diseases.*

Doreen: *Yes, that's what people said. But, you know, the minute Mrs Dunham opened that gate, Patience Frost's old cockerel got livid and chased her away. And right soon after, Mrs Dunham's own geese attacked her. Chased her while she was hanging the washing!*

Joanie: *And she fell into the nettles. That's what I heard!*

Doreen: *She did! She did! And what about that time Mrs Dunham had a plague of bats? It was right soon after. They came and descended on her and hung in the hall and in the rafters, in the shed, everywhere.*

Jean: *God, I hated bats. Mice with wings, they were. I had a phobia about them. They clustered around me when I was on my bike. They tried to get caught up in my hair.*

Doreen: *Yeah, they scared me stiff too. And there were more of them about in those days. And Mrs Dunham, she went round and complained to Mr Lambert the bailiff. He was busy at his beehive, so she had to shout to him from the garden fence. I remember it all. The whole school could hear her. Complaining about them tramps. At the top of her voice. But she wouldn't go near them bees.*

Jean: *God, I was terrified of them.*

Doreen: *Well, we all were, weren't we? Specially afterwards. But there she was, Mrs Dunham, shouting at old man Lambert to get Patience Frost evicted, because of the tramps.*

Molly: *Well, them tramps were a danger, weren't they? They used to give me the creeps.*

Doreen: *Anyway, Mr Lambert left his hive and went round to Patience Frost's cottage. Well, she wouldn't open the door to him! That's what I heard. So he had to bend down and shout through the keyhole. To give her his formal warning about the tramps and the diddycoys. Then he went straight back to his bees.*

Jean: *You know, I watched that beehive once, through Mr Lambert's hedge. I saw them following the queen bee and forming a big cone around her, protecting her.*

Doreen: *I once saw him walking to his outhouse with all them honey bees humming round him. I was terrified, I can tell you! I just knew something was going to happen one day.*

Patience Frost was never evicted from her flint-faced cottage until she was laid to rest in the village churchyard at the age of eighty-five. *Her blameless soul has taken flight,* so reads the tiny epitaph beneath the high trees. And she had continued opening her gate to vagrants. Some villagers still remember her, close to the end, sitting under the laburnum tree, adding her cracked bleat to the canary and the song of a tramp.

A swarm of bees in May is worth a load of hay.
A swarm of bees in June is worth a silver spoon.
A swarm of bees in July isn't worth a fly …

Doreen: *I knew something was going to happen. And it did. Right soon after.*

The Tearoom

Jean: *Remember the trolley Mr Cage the bread man had? With the shafts? He used to pull it himself, all the way from town.*

Doreen: *With them brass lanterns on the back.*

Jean: *They had candles inside, them lanterns. He used to light them up in the wintertime.*

Joanie: *I remember how his bread would still be warm from baking. All crusty and lovely. Cottage loaf, he had. And that bread with the four nobbles on the top. You could pull them off ever so easy. Cobbler, it was called.*

Doreen: *Thursdays, he used to come, Mr Cage the bread man. Thursday afternoons.*

Jean: *Then there was the rag-and-bone man, Mr Joe. He came Fridays.*

Doreen: *He had red paper poppies in his hat, didn't he, Mr Joe? It's funny, we never did know if Joe was his first or his last name.*

Molly: *God, he'd collect anything, Mr Joe – rabbit skins, old clothes, anything. And he'd give Mum a couple of pence for them. He didn't sell, he just bought.*

Jean: *I loved the warm smell of his horse. Remember the big brown horse he used to have?*

Molly: *He'd buy old furniture, any old furniture that was going. And he'd sharpen scissors and knives.*

Jean: *Oh, I can remember that ever so well. He'd make that grindstone spin round. And how those sparks would fly! And Mr Joe, he'd just sit there upright, grinding away. Every Friday he came.*

Doreen: *And Mr Gooch the dairy man came on Thursdays, remember that? He came with a churn, Mr Gooch. Thursday mornings.*

Molly: *You know, I never wanted to drink Mr Gooch's milk. 'Cos his nose was always dripping. Besides, he looked really old to me.*

Doreen: *He had a pint measure and a half-pint one. And Mum would take her jug out to him.*

Jean: *He used to scoop out a little bit more for Mum, didn't he? I think it was 'cos of having all us kids.*

Doreen: *And then he'd go for tea and scone at Mrs Lane's. He'd park his cart next to the brick wall where we used to play.*

All the itinerant traders had their fixed day of the week. During their round, some of them would drop in at the tearoom in Mrs Lane's post office-cum-cottage. In the privacy of The Six Bells, village menfolk assessed the little widow as 'a woman of parts'. Her fine hips and bosom and her strong, neat forearms drew discreet glances from all visitors to the little post room.

Mr Gooch the dairy man, a widower himself, liked to bring wild geraniums for Mrs Lane, and to ladle a little extra milk for her. Mr Cage the bread man, a bachelor of middle age, would bring hydrangeas, and a cottage loaf, warm and crusty.

So, with wild geraniums and hydrangeas, and the constant scent of Mrs Lane's three-cornered scones, the tearoom was a quiet and cosy haven – except when children were out at play.

Doreen: *The hours we used to spend on that brick wall with the boys!*

Jean: *God, I was boy-crazy!* (Singing:)
> *'I like coffee, I like tea,*
> *I like the boys and the boys like me!'*

Doreen: *I was a right flirt. We were always out under them trees.*

Joanie: *We were only allowed out till dark, though.*

Jean: *That chap – that Willy Pepper from The Butts – he fancied you, Joanie.*

Joanie: *What do you want to tell me now for? That's seventy years too late!*

Mrs Lane encouraged dalliance among the young, and indulged their flirtatious games and whooping laughter beneath the trees. What the little postmistress would not tolerate was 'ruffian' behaviour. Only this was known to disturb her own calm and fastidious manners.

Jean: *Tommy and Billy Sturgeon, they set fire to a tree there once, using touchwood. The tree was rotten on the inside,*

*so it was dry. Well, Mrs Lane, she came out and she was
furious! 'Ruffians!' she kept screaming at the boys.
'Shameless ruffians!'*

The post room had a notice board. Behind its wire mesh,
one ancient yellowing page showed the statutory charges
for mail and telegrams. Another announced the closure of
His Majesty's post offices on Lady Day, Midsummer Day,
Michaelmas Day and Christmas Day. Between these official
documents, Mrs Lane pinned up useful homilies:

> A dirty grate makes dinner late.
> Let the ticking clock guide the boiling crock.
> Gluttony kills more than the sword.

Sometimes, the handwritten truisms were replaced by
more ambitious advice:

> Raspberry jam: Take one quart of raspberries to
> 1½ lb of lump sugar …

One Thursday, new information appeared:

> Bread is an important food that fuels our body, to
> help us through the day. The bran inside bread is
> an aid to our digestion.
> Milk is the most valuable of all diets for invalids,
> for they can subsist on it without wasting. A quart
> or more should be given during 24 hours.

Mr Cage the bread man and Mr Gooch the dairy man
studied these facts with mixed reactions. Each was gratified to
see Mrs Lane's good opinion of his commodity. But it was
irritating to see that she had commended the other man's too.

The following Thursday, the notice board brought fresh
advice. But this time, the order had changed: milk first,
bread second:

> To prevent milk boiling over, grease the top inch of the pan with butter. To prevent it from sticking, grease the bottom of the pan with butter.

> Dip old bread in and out of cold water quickly. Bake in a greased tin in a moderate oven till crisp. It will eat like new bread.

Intent and thoughtful were the faces of Mr Gooch the dairy man and Mr Cage the bread man.

The next Thursday, Mr Gooch the dairy man found a new recipe on the notice board:

> Bread-and-butter pudding: Line a dish with butter, then …

Below this, in equally ladylike handwriting, but clearly in second place, was:

> Milk chocolate pudding: Soak ½ oz. of gelatine. Boil a pint of milk …

Mr Gooch the dairy man's face darkened. But, in the little tearoom, a more worrying truth was awaiting him. A brass coach lantern now stood among the hydrangeas on the mantelpiece. Stirring his tea with inelegant force, Mr Gooch the dairy man glared at the shining intruder. An apoplectic shade of red slowly filled his thin face.

Frustration awaited Mr Cage the bread man too. On his next visit, he found a recipe for barley bread displayed below one for milk biscuits. And in the tearoom, a silver milk churn now housed the geraniums in the fireplace. He stared long and hard at the provocative object. As his tea turned cold and his scone lay untouched, a livid pulse began to throb in the brow of Mr Cage the bread man.

Doreen: *Me and Alice Gardner, we saw it all …*

Jean: *You mean that time when …?*

Doreen: *Yes, we saw the whole thing. Well, nearly the whole thing. They were just talking at first, the two of them, next to the brick wall. Their carts were drawn up there, beside each other. And us kids, we weren't really – you know – paying attention. 'Cos they were just, well, talking. But next thing, they were shoving each other. Then, all of a sudden, there they were, on the ground, rolling around, scrapping and clawing at each other. And that's when Mum heard the commotion, and made me come indoors.*

The village had known many foolish men. But few, in the end, advertised their folly so spectacularly as Mr Gooch and Mr Cage. Other witnesses to the shameful little scene reported that Mrs Lane, her face set and tight-lipped, bustled out of the post office, and tried to separate the angry men with a frying pan.

'Ruffians!' she screamed as she swatted at them both. 'Disgraceful ruffians!'

The next day, a Friday, on the back of the rag-and-bone man's cart were the gleaming milk churn and the brass coach lantern. It was the gathered opinion of passers-by that both pieces were sufficiently fine and bright as to turn a fair penny for their new owner.

Fine and bright, too, was the vase of red poppies in the little tearoom. And, for readers of the notice board, fresh words of advice:

One of the most annoying things to encounter when slicing a tomato or dicing an onion is a blunt knife. A well-sharpened knife is a cook's best friend …

The Tinker

Jean: *I loved watching Mr Staveley the blacksmith – all that smoke! And I used to think, those poor horses!, when they were being shod. But I loved watching him at work. Till he got injured, that is.*

Doreen: *Mr Staveley got his leg crushed, didn't he? A horse lunged forward and crushed him against the wall, in the smithy.*

Farming was in a bad way then, with short wages everywhere. But there was money to be made from stoking a furnace and fixing a shoe to a draught horse. So Joe Staveley badly needed a man to help in the smithy till his injury should mend. Very soon, a travelling tinker put himself forward. He had a farrier's hand, he said, so Staveley gave him a trial.

'Oosh, oosh. Hold, girl, hold now …'

In the heat of the smithy, the sweating horse stamped in distress, its eyes bulging. Bent on his crutches, Staveley watched the man at work.

'Good girl, hold now, good girl. Oosh, oosh …'

The huge beast's ears flattened, then it settled and waited, its sides quivering, as the man hammered rhythmically at the black nails.

Terms were agreed on a handshake. After laying out his roll and bundle in Staveley's shed, the tinker stepped back into the smithy and stoked the fire.

Jean: *We saw him sitting by the lake once, didn't we? Mr Staveley's man. When we'd been acorning.*

Doreen: *That's right! And he said to us 'What're you doin' with all them acorns?!'*

Jean: *Yes! And he was a total stranger! God, I was so scared I nearly spilled all my acorns! He frightened me to death!*

Doreen: *Yes, but he was ever so nice to us kids, wasn't he? It was 'cos we told him our mother was poor. Or maybe it was because he knew Dad from the pub.*

Jean: *And he had his pockets stuffed with acorns, remember?*

Doreen: *He did! He pulled 'em out in his hands and showed 'em to us. They brought good luck, he said.*

Jean: *They didn't bring him a lot of luck, did they?*

Molly: *Joanie, remember that time the Chandler boys chased us in the wood, throwing acorns at us?*

Joanie: *That was horse chestnuts!*

Molly: *Horse chestnuts, was it? Well, all I know is: them Chandler boys, they used to chase us and pelt us.*

Joanie: *Mum used to say the Chandler boys'd come to a bad end with their mischief.*

His work done for the day, Staveley's man walked to The
Six Bells for his supper. The men courteously made way for
him so he could have a table to himself for his bread and
cold meat. Later, he ordered more ale and, in the flicker of
the oil lamp, began to tell the men about himself. He had
lost two brothers in the war, he said, but the tinker himself
had been too young to serve. Together with a third brother,
he had set up in farrier work in the county town. But that
brother had fallen foul of the magistrates in the tithes
revolt, and was in prison now. So here he sat, a homeless
tinker, robbed of a living in his own land.

His audience listened uncomfortably and did not speak.
Finally, he ceased his talking. He drew out a handful of
acorns and sat fingering them at his table, deep in thought.

The next night, the tinker took more ale than supper,
and became strident.

'Look around you! Look at your lives!' The men
huddled in the lamplight, eyeing their tankards. 'A land fit
for heroes! Just look! Look at the gentry and their grand
estates and their pheasants and stables, and tell me what's
changed! We've been fooled! Fooled and betrayed!'

His gaze moved from face to face. But not one pair of
eyes met his own.

'First the generals bungled the war, then the politicians
bungled the peace! I tell you we've been betrayed!'

Doreen: *But people weren't interested in politics, were
they? Not in the village. Well, Dad wasn't. I don't think
anyone was.*

Molly: *Dad, he was just interested in horse racing and
beer. That's all Dad cared about.*

'Look around you!' The tinker slapped the table with
his open palm and glared at the silent faces. Words like
'socialism' and 'solidarity' crept into his fierce tirade. But

they fell on flint, and were met with bent shoulders and lowered faces.

Suddenly he gave up, and slumped in the shadows, scrunching the acorns in his pocket, and fuming.

The real trouble began in the next parish.

Word got around that building had started at the Hall there, and that old man Blunston was ready to hire out horses, wagons and men for the job. But the builder wanted to use his own labourers – men not accustomed to animals, it was said. They were willing to do the haulage and work the horses in return for their building wage.

That evening, the tinker stormed into The Bells, his face grim. He picked at his supper in the lamp's yellow glow. Then, as the men glanced at him sideways, he sat staring at the floor. The landlord – a haggard, gaunt-eyed man – tried to busy himself in the growing unease.

Then, of a sudden, the tinker slammed down his tankard and clambered to his feet. He glared at one of the men: a short, balding creature with a thin face.

'You're Blunston's farrier, ain't you? What're you goin' to do?'

The little fellow hunched over his tankard, gripping it with both hands.

'Stand up to him, man!' the tinker shouted, 'I'll join you! We'll refuse our labour! What d'you say?'

Scenting danger, the anxious landlord stepped in.

'All right now. No mischief here, if you please!'

The tinker turned to him, blinking.

'Mischief?' he repeated incredulously. '*Mischief?!*'

Jean: *Mum and Dad never discussed politics, did they? But Dad was a Tory. I'm sure he was. He'd vote Tory just because it was the right and proper thing to do. You'd never catch him getting mixed up with anything like Socialism. He was all for everyone in their place, King and Country, the gentry and the rest, accepting authority.*

Doreen: *Same with Mum. She was a Conservative. Not that she ever mentioned a word about it. But she went around to the village hall to vote. And she just wanted everything as it should be, everything and everybody in their place, the rich people in their houses and us in ours.*

Molly: *Joanie, remember that skipping song? 'Let us love our occupations ...'*

Molly/Joanie (together):

> *'... Bless the Squire and his relations,*
> *Strive to meet our obligations,*
> *Always know our proper stations!'*

Joanie (laughing): *We learned that in Sunday school, didn't we?! Well, fancy us remembering that!*

Molly: *There, you see, my dear. We're not as far gone as we thought!*

In the shade of the stables, old Blunston stood frowning at his boots and slapping his thigh with a hunting crop. At his side, the thin-faced farrier spoke quietly, making quick chopping motions of the hand. The old man nodded from time and time, his eyes still on his boots.

He who holds the land holds power.

The ancient first law of the village asserted itself. Dust settled on the roll and bundle in the shed beside the smithy. Men and women murmured 'good riddance', and bent to their labour in fields and stables and homes and hovels. And the tinker took his place in the long sad carnival of gypsies, day labourers, tramps and vagrants, menders and pickers, beggars with tin cans, ragged men and wives peddling dolls and trinkets and pegs: all the landless creatures who had touched the life of the village and never left a mark.

Joanie: *Remember we went to the lake soon after and saw acorns on the water? They were bobbing on the surface. Just floating. I always wondered how they got there.*

Molly: *I reckon it was them Chandler boys. They was always up to mischief.*

Seedcake

Jean: *Remember Colonel Pugh? He used to walk the whole length of the village, lifting his hat to ladies on his way to church.*

Doreen: *He was very posh, wasn't he, Colonel Pugh? Very well spoken and well dressed. He came from quite a wealthy family, I think. He had a sister with an estate in Scotland.*

With his upright bearing and fine Edwardian manners, the Colonel presented a stirring sight during his Sunday progress. At the church, he would greet his housekeepers, Miss Sarah and Miss Anne, as elaborately as if they had not met for weeks.

Calm and spacious behind its high brick wall, Colonel Pugh's home – the Big House – was a treasury of Regency furniture, artefacts and paintings. They were tributes to the cultivated taste of the Colonel's late wife. And it was she who had had the flush toilet installed – possibly the first in the village, although there is no strict record of this.

> Joanie: *I used to clean at the Big House. And, I can tell you, I wasn't allowed to use that loo. Well, actually, I don't remember being forbidden to use it. But I knew it wasn't allowed. It wasn't allowed to sit on the chairs either, or on the bed, or open any of the cupboards. When I cleaned over at the Rectory, I always made sure I spent a penny, so I could flush it away. That was luxury. I didn't do it at the Big House, though.*

A veteran of campaigns from Pretoria to the Somme, the Colonel was a robust man who took vigorous morning walks. In the afternoons, he retired to his library, selected a leather-bound Dickens or Trollope, and settled into his high-backed Regency chair beneath the chandelier. Then he would fall asleep, the book open and unread on his lap.

He allowed himself one weekly lapse, which was as regimentally fixed as his walk to church. Every Friday night, the Colonel went 'on the razzle'. This meant fetching four bottles of beer from the cellar, telephoning an old army comrade and reminiscing over past adventures until their brains became slumbrous.

> Joanie: *That was the only telephone I ever saw in the village. It looked dangerous to me, that big black thing! I used to skirt around it when I was cleaning. And Saturday mornings, I had to empty his piddle bottle. He was too lazy to go to the loo! It was a stone bottle with a spout to put his doodle in. He wouldn't empty that bottle himself, lazy old bugger! And he did a lot of wee. I think he drank a lot those Friday nights.*

The slaughter of men in the Great War had created a surplus of rural spinsters, of whom Miss Anne and Miss Sarah were part. Not much was known about them in the village, for they were private ladies of a very English breed. Their age, origin and financial circumstances were known to themselves and the Lord, but to no one else. They appeared to have adequate means, though, and probably did not depend on the Colonel's employ.

> Joanie: *One of them told me once that working in the Big House with all those paintings was 'part of Life's Rich Tapestry'. I remember those words ever so well. 'Part of Life's Rich Tapestry,' she said. But, 'course, I wasn't interested in anything like that. Mum just sent me there for the earnings.*

> Jean: *Those ladies, those housekeepers, they worked at the Big House – ooh, for years. Ever since I could remember. They talked very posh – a bit like the Colonel, really. But they were nice, not snooty.*

It was said they had been travelling companions to royalty, but such stories were always being dreamed up in the village. What is known is that they were voluntary midwives and, as such, honorary members of the Mothers Union.

> Jean: *They used to cycle to those meetings every Wednesday, remember? And they always took some seedcake with them.*

> Doreen: *That's right! Do you remember those upright bikes they had? With the baskets for packing the seedcake in? They baked a lot of seedcake.*

Oblivious to the new *Highway Code*, Miss Anne and Miss Sarah would pedal side by side, occupying the full breadth of the road. In those more tranquil days, they never once took harm on their journey, and the seedcake was always brought safely to table at the meeting house.

In the cottage that was their home, the ladies' existence was one of untroubled tempo and simple pleasures. Every day, Miss Sarah would find an hour on her rocking chair at the fireside and read a tale of adventure and romance in *The People's Friend*. She would gaze happily at the line drawings of firm-jawed young men wooing porcelain young ladies, or rescuing them from hot-blooded Arabs in burning deserts.

While Miss Sarah was among the cushions of her rocking chair, Miss Anne would be seated in the outhouse. There, she browsed through the paper squares into which last week's issue of *The People's Friend* had been cut. The squares, which hung on a string, served two essential purposes, one of them being to facilitate Miss Anne's unique style of reading. She would study an illustrated paragraph here, a portion of severed chapter there. Then she tried to guess at the plot, the romantic intrigue and the missing parts of the story. This provided deep pleasure and a spur to the imagination. Indeed, the ladies were continually reminding each other how reading was a vital part of Life's Rich Tapestry.

Their cottage was just three hundred yards from the Big House. In the course of the week, in their wide bustle skirts, Miss Sarah and Miss Anne trod the distance many times. At eleven in the morning, they waddled over to prepare the Colonel's luncheon in his scullery. At the stroke of noon, it would be on the dining table beneath a white serviette, and the Colonel would arrive through the front door at the same moment. Bowing theatrically, he would enquire as to their welfare. The unvarying ritual called on them to report some news from the village and the Colonel to mention the health of his sister in Perthshire. Then:

'Don't let your luncheon get cold, Colonel!' Miss Anne would utter her French phrase – '*Bon appétit!*' – and the ladies would withdraw.

They returned in the late afternoon to lay out bread, cold meat, chutney, milk, a slice of seedcake and another white serviette. The season permitting, a tomato or some cucumber might also appear. Then Miss Sarah would peep into the library to study the householder. Asleep in the high-backed chair, his book open on his knees, he would present a picture of cherubic health and elegant repose. Miss Sarah would glance with interest, too, at the opulence of chandelier, deep-pile carpet and framed portraits.

At the same time, Miss Anne would visit the toilet to replenish the white serviettes there, and to shift any china ornament which required realignment. Then, before withdrawing, she would gaze in fascination at the luxury of the marble commode, its silver chain and the cistern of eggshell-blue enamel.

One day, the Colonel declared that he was going up to London for the weekend, for his Brigade reunion.

'I am confident, ladies,' he announced trustingly, 'that I may leave the premises in your capable hands.'

Miss Sarah and Miss Anne sensed at once that life had opened to them a new strand of its Rich Tapestry.

> Joanie: *When I got to the Big House that Saturday, the two ladies were sort of – well, excited. They seemed bright-eyed and bouncy, if you know what I mean. And they got started on me straight away.*

'My dear … what was your name again?' enquired Miss Anne, 'Ah, Joan. But, of course. Well, Joan …' – she lowered her voice to a pious tremor – 'we have served. We have served long and nobly. Now the Colonel is away, on a special razzle. So the Lord has laid in our path an opportunity – an opportunity which it is our duty – our *Christian* duty – to seize.'

'Discretion, my dear,' murmured Miss Sarah. 'Discretion is all.'

> Joanie: *'Course, I was glad I didn't have any bottle to empty. But those women – they were talking in riddles! I had no idea what they were on about. So I just went and busied myself cleaning the grate. Next thing, one of them had gone into the library, and the other had toddled off to the loo! Well, I was surprised, 'course I was. But I was only – what? – twelve, so I didn't ask any questions.*

After just ten minutes, the ladies were back. They stood gazing at one other across the table, crestfallen and still.

There is no record of events beyond one person's frail memory. But we may suppose that the Colonel's library seat did not prove comfortable for Miss Sarah. Its rigid frame may have provided less ease than her rocking chair and rag cushions. Not only this – despite the splendour of chandelier and rich furnishing, the library had no fireplace. So perhaps, finally, it seemed drab and spartan, and lacking the friendly embers and homely crack of the burning log.

And there may have been a literary difficulty too. Spine-ribbed leather books with close print and no pictures had their place. But they could be found wanting when compared with the appeal of *The People's Friend.*

And what of Miss Anne? Well, she was among those villagers who, during sedentary exertions, were accustomed to the hard grain and edge of English oak. For such a person suddenly to be on polished marble brought the worry and danger of slippage.

Then there was the circumference of the Big House commode. While fitting in every sense for a retired cavalry officer, it could not have offered the best convenience for a more spacious user. And – as with Miss Sarah, so with Miss Anne – there was the reading dilemma. To a person who took pleasure in assembling fragments of illustrated text, blank serviettes may have proved dull and unrewarding.

The ladies gazed at each other dolefully. Miss Anne was the first to speak, in a tone of quiet reasonableness.

'We have tried, Sarah. And I am glad. I am truly glad.'

'All part of Life's Rich Tapestry, Anne' – Miss Sarah's words were measured and calm – 'I would not have missed it for the world.'

They turned to the figure kneeling at the black-leaded grate.

'My dear, remember,' murmured one, 'well-bred ladies are always discreet.'

'Would you like a slice of seedcake?' asked the other.

Miss Flack

Joanie: *She used to be dressmaker to lords and ladies, Miss Flack. That's what I heard. But she had those bad joints.*

Jean: *It was arthritis, is what it was. Sometimes, she used to take bee stings against it. That's what Mum said.*

Doreen: *Do you remember we saw some posh people come once, Jean? For measuring and fitting.*

Jean: *I do. I remember that.*

Doreen: *She had a muddly house, Miss Flack, but it was lovely and cosy. With a big chair. She was a clever needlewoman. She made me a jacket – plain brown.*

Joanie: *She made me a skirt.*

Jean: *She didn't like it, though, having to live next to a houseful of kids. Not when we first moved in. All us kids next door. She thought we'd be a rowdy family.*

Doreen: *Well, brother Jack, he was dead frightened of her at first, when we moved in. It's funny how they warmed to each other, him and Miss Flack. For a while, anyway.*

None of the sisters know quite how it started, that fleeting companionship shared by their brother and the spinster dressmaker. But they remember it was the time of the long snow.

Doreen: *The schoolroom was flooded, wasn't it? 'Cos the pipes had burst. So we had to stay at home. That lasted for – ooh, for ages.*

Jean: *Mum didn't mind that at all – having us girls at home. Not with all the scrubbing and mending and peeling to be done.*

Joanie: *And all that wet washing hanging indoors. God, I hated it!*

Jean: *But we had our uses, didn't we? She put us to work, did Mum. Not that little sod Jack, though. She couldn't wait to get him out of the house!*

So, somehow, Jack found himself having tea and Swiss roll in Miss Flack's cosy, muddly home. With its thin entrail of red jam, the Swiss roll was the driest thing the boy had ever tasted. But he chewed it dutifully, as he turned the pages of *The Bumper Annual for Boys*. He carried the book everywhere, but never actually read it. Jack was always being chided for his poor reading.

Doreen: *He wasn't very good at school, was he, Jack? He left in Standard 4.*

Jean: *Well, he couldn't cope with it, could he? He was always asking me questions and trying to get me to help him.*

Molly: *He had to go home with chilblains once.*

Jack liked to pick out a black-and-white drawing in the book and to study it long and silently. He was bent over one – the huddled shape of a man staggering in a snowstorm – when Miss Flack joined him at the table. She peered at the picture, then read aloud the title of the story.

'A Very Gallant Gentleman.' Then: 'Would you like to hear it?'

Jack nodded. So, crouched at the flames of the tiny log fire, the woman read the tragic story of Scott's polar expedition and the self-sacrifice of Captain Oates. Here and there, a phrase caught her fancy and she carefully repeated it in her frail monotone: '... ever spurred by hope ... there beat an English heart ... splendid in the face of death ...'

The boy listened, entranced.

That night, as fresh snow hurled itself about the land, Jack dreamed of the crippled Oates and the harsh purity of the blizzard which had consumed him. The Englishman's last words turned over and over in the boy's brain.

'I am just going outside and may be some time.'

Next day, Miss Flack offered to read another tale. Jack chose 'The Lost Hamlet' this time, because the picture showed a square church tower like the one in the village.

In the story, a geological rift had plunged an English hamlet deep into a valley, bounded by high black cliffs. Cut off from the world, its stout-hearted inhabitants continued doggedly with their work and their lives. But time passed them by, so they knew nothing of aeroplanes, or the wireless, or talking-picture houses, or of the great cataclysm which had seized and shattered the world.

At the end of the tale, the woman paused and repeated the last sentence slowly: 'Nurtured by an English sun, the hamlet lives and will be found.'

For a long time, woman and boy sat and gazed into the lapping flames.

That night, as the snow thudded against the windowpane, Jack dreamed of the white-coated forgotten homes, and heard the church bell echoing against the walls of the valley. And he pictured himself, lurching into the teeth of a blizzard, as the dark, mighty rocks towered over him. But the snow was so blinding and so vast that the cliffs were obliterated. And, soon, it effaced the whole world, and scourged it away, leaving only Jack, lone and heroic, pressing forward to his fate in the white storm.

The snow had drifted up against Miss Flack's door during the night. So Jack had to work and shovel before he could let himself in.

Immediately, they began talking of the lost hamlet, as the boy had hoped they would. The woman asked his opinion. Did he think the hamlet would have an Institute, like the one in their own village? Jack thought it must have, and Miss Flack agreed. Did it have a post office too? And a shop? They agreed that it must.

They stopped talking and gazed into the fire. Then:

'They know nothing of the war,' she smiled at him. 'It passed them by.'

But Jack was thinking of the shop. He hoped it would sell real Swiss roll, with thick red jam between the layers, not like the brittle, dry thing on his plate.

He looked up, to find her still smiling, with bent creases in her cheeks. There would be a field too, she said, where Jack would play for the cricket team. Her brother would like to play too.

'Edmund is his name,' she said and nodded brightly.

But Jack knew the harsh, dangerous clang of bat and ball, and had seen the blacksmith's bruised knuckles after a mishap in a cricket game.

Jean: *He was terrified of anything, our Jack. An oak tree would frighten him in the moonlight. He'd think it was a living thing with waving arms, ready to attack him.*

Doreen: *And he was terrified of you, Jean. You were a right bully!*

Jean: *Well, he was easy to frighten, that Jack. He coughed up some phlegm once, and I warned him he was coughing his brains up. God, he was frightened to death!*

In a world of provocation and dangers and cackling, taunting sisters, the boy was ever ready to retreat to the shelter of his dreamworld. So he gave himself heart and soul to the invention of the lost hamlet. And he was led on by the woman's quiet certitude. For, as they added one fantastic detail after another, she did not waver at any point.

So it was that the smithy did not have workhorses like the village ones, with huge heads that rocked and slavered, and shoes of iron which kicked dangerous lighted sparks. Instead, there were foals, which a boy could stroke and feed. Likewise, the lake acquired a bank of mud, where Miss Flack could cure her arthritic joints, and where Jack would catch leaping, bright-chested newts.

'Edmund will go fishing with you.'

Jack looked at her, irritated. What did fishing have to do with newts?

Then the dark creases in Miss Flack's cheeks hardened. The hamlet would have a doctor, she said, no charlatan, but a real doctor with proper medicine. She rubbed her knotted hands on her thighs and glared balefully into the fire.

That night, Jack dreamed he walked alone in the snowbound hamlet, steady-eyed, calm, ready to sacrifice heart, sinew and life itself in a single selfless act.

But someone, an intruder, a grown-up, was lurking in the shadow of the dream, invisible, but waiting, waiting to steal the boy's heroic deed.

*   *   *

Next morning, the snowdrift had disappeared. The village still groaned beneath the white mass, but thin grey rivulets had begun to inch down the dressmaker's window. The boy saw her, asleep in the big chair as the flames curled around the log in the grate. Lifting the door latch, he eased himself in.

She was emitting a small clucking sound, as if something had caught in her throat. Should he turn and leave? But where could he go, except home again, next door? There, he would surely be scolded for getting under his mother's feet. Or his sisters, in their boredom, would find a way to taunt him or make him cry. So he wandered around the woman's cluttered room, the book under his arm, his eyes roving.

A flat, sharp-edged object caught his attention. It rested beneath a pile of fabrics and sewing materials on the woman's worktable. He found that it was a picture frame, with a folded paper wedged in it. With a covert glance at the woman, the boy tugged the paper free.

He had seen a telegram before, at Aunt Nelly's. A telegram was to tell you somebody was dead. The boy fingered the paper's rough edge and ran his thumb over its black War Office crest. Then he studied the picture: a young man in sepia, smiling, and wearing the cap of a military officer.

The boy's swift eye picked out the dark creases in the man's cheeks. Then he turned to the lonely, broken-hearted woman and saw her for the first time.

As the rays of pale sun filtered into the room, he imagined the snow thawing on the rooves of the lost hamlet. And he pictured the church melting, and the street, and the smithy, and the houses and the high rocks and the passing into white nothing of the whole fantastic dream. Then he trod his way to the door and waited.

With more throaty clucking, the woman climbed from sleep. Her eyes settled on the watery sunlight as she massaged her hands on her thighs and brushed away some crumbs of Swiss roll. Then she saw the boy.

'Well, I never,' she murmured.

The Bumper Annual for Boys beneath his arm, he grasped the last melting thread of the dream.

'I am just going outside,' he said, 'and may be some time.'

The Mermaid

Doreen: *He was an odd one, brother Billy.*

Joanie: *We used to say he'd got rover's blood, didn't we? From Mum's side.*

Jean: *Well, that's what we said. But he was a strange child.*

Billy gazed entranced at the wonderful thing. Body, undercarriage, horse shafts, wheel spokes – every inch was painted in gorgeous, flowing blends of indigo, maroon, emerald, crimson and cream.

At the open door of the caravan stood the cobbler in green corduroy trousers – a bold contrast to the grey serge worn about the village. Shyly, the boy handed him the cloth bag and the sixpence, then watched the man's creased-leather face as he took out the shoes and studied them. Without a word, he turned and mounted the wooden steps.

As the man's cutting and hammering began, Billy wandered around the caravan, examining its painted gossamer herons and the emerald waves stretched along its ribs. Metalware hung from hooks on the sides: a kettle, green-striped buckets, a tin bath. At the rear, a mermaid in a mosaic of beads studded the entire breadth of the wagon, her hair cascading in creamy swathes. A stovepipe chimney stood companion to a tiny flagpole which bore the red-and-white banner of Saint George.

A woman emerged, her ropes of hair tied in a purple band. Wrist bangles glinted as she tossed a pan of water over the cinders of a campfire. She glanced at the boy with dark, foreign eyes.

That evening, at home, Billy laid down his whittling knife and carved stick and studied the tight bun of his mother's hair. Then he pictured the untrammelled waves of the mermaid and the cobbler woman's coarse black strands – hair blacker than any Billy had seen. And he caught again the silent flash of the cobbler woman's eyes.

A movement from the scullery broke his thoughts. He found his father staring at him. The man's fleshy, resentful gaze seemed to fill the room, to clutch and choke the very air.

Doreen: *They never spoke much to each other, did they? Dad and Bill?*

Joanie: *Well, Bill, he couldn't even look Dad in the face.*

Jean: *And Dad hated him being so timid. Remember when he tried to make him take up the well-sinking work? Bill just couldn't stomach it.*

Joanie: *You're right. Those tools of Dad's, those grappling irons he used for hoisting – they used to make Bill really ill.*

Doreen: *He was clever with his hands, though, wasn't he, Bill? With carving. He was good at woodwork. Remember the little stool he made for Mum?*

Jean: *Dad burned that in the end, didn't he, that stool? He just dumped it on the bonfire in the garden, where he burned all the rubbish.*

Molly: *Sometimes, it seemed they really hated each other, Dad and Bill.*

Joanie: *They couldn't get on at all, could they?*

Lowering his eyes, the father fumbled for his pocket watch. 'Not long now,' he grunted. But the girls were already jostling around the great wireless set, ready for the crackling ritual of the six o'clock news.

'It has been announced that His Majesty the King is suffering from a cold with some fever ...' – the words were reverent, mournful – '... and is remaining in bed ...'

Next day, Billy was watching the cobbler at work when, suddenly, the man laid aside his hammer, leather strips and nails. He winked at the boy and, bending from his iron last, dragged out a flat carved box with a hand crank. Turning it, the cobbler watched the boy with smiling eyes as the tiny harpsichord notes of 'Goodbye Dolly Gray' jangled the air. Then the woman appeared. With a dainty rocking of the head and fluttering wrists and fingers, she weaved about the grass in front of the caravan. Her eyebrows flashed a silent invitation to the boy. But Billy, smiling and swaying at the cobbler's side, did not join the dance.

'His Majesty has passed a restless night, owing to persistence of the fever. There is some congestion of the lung.' Billy and his sisters stared at each other. Their mother, her face crumpled in dismay, covered her mouth with her hands.

Doreen: *People used to get really upset about anything like that, like the King being ill.*

Jean: *I can remember the King's illness. It lasted for ages.*

Penny a Look, Tuppence a Feel

Doreen: *Mum got really upset about it. Everybody did.*

Next day, Billy found the door of the caravan closed. At his knock, the woman silently opened it, put a finger to her lips and shook her head. The aroma of goose fat seeped from inside the caravan, reminding the boy of the dreadful time when Aunt Trudy was fading away. He turned and walked home slowly, staring at the ground.

'The King has passed another restless night ...' – the family huddled over the huge contraption, catching its faint phrases – '... a slight extension of mischief in the lung ...' Then the thin, sombre message was too weak to hear.

Joanie: *Remember how we had to press our ears against that wireless? To catch the sounds when it was fading? God, I hated that. I'd get right annoyed!*

Doreen: *It was the accumulators. It had to be loaded with accumulators, remember?*

Joanie: *When that damned thing started to fade ...*

Doreen: *They were heavy, those accumulators. Sort of square, with a handle. Dad used to get them from the garage.*

Hearing that the cobbler was poorly, Mother sent Billy with a can of pea soup and a dumpling.

'You thank her heartily and right obliged for the kindness ...' – the cobbler woman's voice was rough-edged, dusky – '... and mind you say it proper now.' She wagged a finger and made Billy repeat the words. The boy could hear the cobbler's chesty wheeze inside the caravan, reminding him again of Aunt Trudy.

Side by side, the cobbler woman and Billy sat and listened to 'Goodbye Dolly Gray', until the doleful metal chords sagged and petered into stillness among the bare trees.

* * *

At six o'clock, the family gathered and bent to hear the faltering words from the wireless: '... the King ... increase of the fever ... restless night ...'

The village congregation prayed for the ailing monarch, but Billy sent up his prayer for the cobbler. He willed the entreaty forward, tried to channel it through the stained glass before him. The boy chafed and worried. How would his wordless thoughts ever penetrate the imprisoning, lead-bound window? Or find a path through the confining Holy Cross and into the November sky, where God waited?

Billy pressed his head on the cold edge of the pew and tried to shut away the echoing nave. Shut away the Sadler girls, giggling beside him and peeping through their fingers. Shut away the village, its inert, cloddish soil and grey, ghostly barns, and the straddling beams of his home, his father's cold eyes and sullen jowls and the grey, flaking room where Aunt Trudy had choked her last. Away the grim, heavy-handled tools, and the black well in the garden that would seize a boy and drown him dead.

Eyes tight shut, he opened his mind to the lawless blaze of colours on the caravan, the cobbler woman's elfin dance beneath the beech trees, the brilliant lines of herons and the mermaid's oceanic hair.

That evening, the news lurched out in spasms, like Aunt Trudy's trapped gasps on the night she died: '... His Majesty ... operation ... drainage ... right side of the chest ... critical hours ...' Then the wireless fell silent.

Billy stood motionless, gazing up at the black trees. He imagined the notes of 'Dolly Gray' as cold, invisible pearls clinging to the skeletal branches. Then, for a long time, he stared at the cinders and the churned ruts where the caravan had been.

His face folded in dismay, Bill trudged back to the grey cottage.

* * *

Blossoms fluttered about the land and clung in myriad thousands to the hedgerows. Flocks of lambs, frantic for the protection of lost mothers, wobbled on stick legs, wailing plaintively. Blackbirds, their beaks stuffed with twigs, busied themselves with the building of their new homes. Thrushes, bouncing on the damp earth, listened with cocked heads for the stirring of worms.

There was no place for the cobbler in Billy's thoughts now, nor for the silver mermaid, nor the music box. No place for the King of England, recuperating in his far-off haven by the sea. No place but for wrestling fights, and raucous cricket on the green, and for rabbits – darting, sharp-eared targets for catapults and sticks – and for the Sadler girls, whose taunting calls and browned limbs maddened him and tangled all his thoughts.

And then, one rainy afternoon, came new accumulators and, with them, the forgotten voice of the world beyond:

'This is the six o'clock news ...'

National Debt. Stricken coalfields. Workless men in shipyards. The royal baby Elizabeth. The launch of an airship. A new home for ex-servicemen. A Boy Scouts' jamboree. And, suddenly one Wednesday, from Buckingham Palace: '... gratitude for the affectionate welcome received on returning from his long months of illness ...'

Billy's memory stirred. Wide-eyed, he stared at his sisters, then rose to his feet and walked to the window. A breeze sprang up and flowed through the sycamore tree at the roadside. '... A wonderful crowd gave the King a tumultuous welcome ...'

As the boy's mind turned, a premonition took shape. His senses on fire, he rushed from the house and up the wooded lane, to the beech trees. And there, among the silent hanging notes of 'Dolly Gray', Billy waited.

The cavalcade arrived at dusk. Ribboned horses, their manes tied with gaudy rags. Caravans bright with scarlet streaks and angel lamps and oak-leaf carvings. Rooves glistening with ironware and trinkets in garish shuttered cases. Brass kettles, stoves, drums of oil and baths of silver zinc, clanging gently on brilliant painted walls. And, last in the gorgeous convoy, the wagon with the flag of Saint George and the stovepipe chimney.

The travellers pitched their camp in the dying of the sun. Tallow candles flickered in doorways and tethered goats nuzzled at bushes in shadow. In the light of the campfire, laughing, brown-skinned women in beads and bracelets eased their shoulders to the surge of accordion and flute and tin spoons. Men drank from painted stone flagons and wiped their lips with kerchieves and joked in a strange melodic tongue. And around the fire, children – six or seven of them, tousle-haired, quicksilver, foreign, their eyes and teeth glittering in the firelight – leapt like tigers, flung their arms and whooped to the magic of the dance.

Sitting cross-legged beside the cobbler, Billy burned with a daring wish to join the hurly-burly and throw himself among the prancing, black-haired children. But he did not join the dance.

Next day, the travellers bartered their wares at the doors of the village: beads and pegs, wooden toys and tin charms, heather and corn dolls with small round heads. And then they were gone, departed as lightly as they had come, roamers and vagabonds winding their way through the land.

Billy did not see them go. But he felt the pull of their leaving, sensed the racing of devils and pagan, rootless tribes. Hill-topped horizons and the ribbon of the long road murmured to his rover's heart. And he heard the wild rhapsody in places where kings held no sway.

But he could not join the dance.

Joanie: *I remember that stool Billy made. It had a mermaid on it.*

Doreen: *It did. Billy carved that himself. A mermaid with long hair.*

Jean: *He was a strange child, though, our Billy. Never was able to settle, was he?*

Doctor Harveys

Doreen: *He had to take care of his brother, did Mr Herod. That's what Mum told me. 'Cos his brother was an invalid, she said. Mr Herod had to take care of him – ooh, for ever such a long time.*

Joanie: *I liked Mr Herod the gamekeeper. Everyone liked Mr Herod. He had a nice, fresh face.*

Doreen: *He did garden work for the surgeon's widow, didn't he? Well, for a while.*

At the sound of the pigeon's throbbing weep, Jack Herod looked up.

As always, it evoked that September day when he had last seen Tommy Nunn. But nowadays, Jack didn't fall to brooding whenever he heard the pigeon's call. That was over and past, he could tell himself.

He paused in his labours this time, though, and thought of Tommy. And of brother Will. He pictured them sitting side by side on the station platform, in khaki and boots, their shoulders bristling with the brass insignia of the county regiment. And imitating birdsongs: the pigeon's melancholy bleat, the chattering of long-tailed tits, the shrilling finch, the blackbird's rapid, scolding alarm ...

The yelp of the small owl.

Jack's face clouded.

Ah, but it was over, he told himself, staring at the ground. Over and long past. Many and often had been the times when the call of a bird had torn his heart and rekindled the old bitter hurt. But that was all past now, and the years had wended their way.

So, as the pigeon poured out its sadness, Jack continued his scything of the widow's cow parsley. He looked up at the porch and caught her still, feline poise as she sat reading at the table in her grey shawl. Her strange, fluting accent rang in his mind, and the odd stressing of her words.

Doreen: *She was a mystery woman, wasn't she, the surgeon's widow? We only ever saw her in church. We just called her the surgeon's widow.*

Jean: *She seemed foreign, didn't she? She had that way about her. I reckon she thought she was somebody, but I don't think anyone really knew her.*

Doreen: *I remember when her husband – the surgeon – died. It was right soon after they came to the village. I remember the hearse going down the road and everyone closing their curtains, like they used to do.*

Leaning on his scythe, Jack found that the memory of Tommy Nunn was not to be shaken off lightly. He recalled the long-ago day when he and Tommy had conspired to sabotage a shoot on the estate. Seven years old, they were, or eight: they'd risen before the dawn and taken Tommy's mongrel hound out to the woods, to raise the long-tailed birds, and send them, honking and clattering, safe from the coming slaughter of the guns.

Now, with the long years of hindsight, Jack could smile a bitter smile at his and Tommy's disastrous naivety. For one thing, the semi-tamed birds refused to be flushed from their woodland haven. For another, it wasn't very long before the boys were caught by the enraged gamekeeper and marched back to the estate house at the barrel of his gun.

Of course, they always had to learn the hard way, the boys. They got the hiding of their lives, the dog was summarily shot and the lads' fathers came perilously close to losing their work on the estate.

But, Jack reflected ruefully, firm and true was the bond that held him and Tommy Nunn after that painful day.

His memory drifted back to the station platform, and to Tommy and brother Will polishing their apples. Jack's throat lurched as he pictured Will biting into the acidic flesh, his eyes thin and intent.

He looked up again at the still shape of the widow at her table in the porch. And he thought again of the day he had met her in the village, and shown her the Doctor Harveys in his sack. She had peered dubiously at their dark-stained skins.

Bake a Doctor Harvey apple and it became sugary, he could have told her. It kept for a week, sometimes longer, and provided a sweetmeat to sustain a man who was only half-alive. This, too, Jack had learned the hard way. But, of course, he had told her nothing of this.

'No worry about them skins, ma'am,' he smiled, 'you'll eat a peck of dirt before you're dead.'

Their eyes had met as she bobbed her head in assent. And Jack's heart had been taken.

So he had looked to himself, assessed his potential as a companion and provider. Of course, there'd been no chance for courting while Will was still half-alive. And nor for a good while after that, for Jack himself had been a stricken man. But if the six arduous years of caring for Will had any meaning, they'd shown that Jack could fend and forage for two.

So a notion had taken root in his mind. He had sought out Saint Valentine's Day in his almanac. Then he had placed the open book by his bed, and bided his time. And now the day had dawned.

Jack saw the widow look up from her table and gaze quizzically towards the village. He bent to his work again and continued raking her flinty soil, till she got up and left.

Then, bearing his sack, he quietly made his way to the porch. Entering, he placed the sack on the woman's cane table. Then, carefully, he emptied out the ten bold winter apples from his fine-bearing Doctor Harvey tree. Next, with a calm, deliberate hand, Jack arranged them into the form of a Valentine's heart.

As he turned to leave, his glance fell on the book resting on the widow's seat. Though no reading man, he was caught by the un-English wording of its title. And the ornate brown cover bore the crest of a spread eagle, clutching a black hooked cross.

He lifted the book. Opening it at random, he found a rough-tinted picture of youthful drummers and buglers in uniform. They seemed to be on the march. Above them hung a flag with the same dark hooked cross.

He turned the page: more boys, in black leather shorts and brown shirts and knee socks. The picture showed them gathered on a station platform, eager-faced, gazing down the track …

Jack stared out at the garden, his senses reeling.

He saw again the grinning boy that had been Tommy Nunn, saw him haul the lumpy grey kitbag from platform to train, saw Tommy turn and wave. And then Tommy was gone – blown to pieces in a crater of mud, they said. His tongue and eyes and all his swift thought, blown to pieces, and the visceral net of his flesh and nerve, the grain of his bones and teeth, and Tommy's every dream and trilling song.

Will had returned, though. On his twenty-second birthday, he had been trundled home on Mr Bonney's cart and laid in the shade of the Doctor Harvey apple tree.

'My birthday gift.' So Will called his burden of the six harsh years to come. Jack always rewarded the whispered joke with a grim, supportive smile. For, in the language of the enemy, *gift* meant 'poison'. And Will had seen the yellow shells falling softly at Ypres.

Jack looked again at the book in his hands and turned another page: helmeted soldiers at a wheeled cannon, gripping metal canisters ...

He pictured again the face of his brother, groping on his knees at the bedside. Heard again his brother's yelp, mimicking the frantic cry of the small owl. Saw a man, his bronchial tubes stripped of membrane, still choking, struggling for life, years after the yellow shells had burst.

Slowly, Jack replaced the book on the cane seat exactly as he had found it. Then, with heavy and deliberate purpose, he re-gathered the shining Doctor Harveys, one by one.

When he reached Will's graveside, Jack stooped and carefully laid the apples in a cluster on the grassy mound. Then, with measured care, he lifted his boot and ground them, crushed them into the soil, churned into pulp their white flesh and all their yellow skin.

Then Jack stepped back and watched, stone-faced and silent, until the last of the astringent, foaming juice had drained to the earth, and joined the poisoned remains of his brother.

Jean: *I don't suppose anyone really knew if she was foreign, the surgeon's widow.*

Doreen: *Oh, I expect Mr Herod knew. He did garden for her.*

Joanie: *She was a strange lady, wasn't she? I reckon she never got over losing her husband, so soon after they'd moved to the village.*

Doreen: *She became very strange in the end. I remember that.*

The Row

Jean: *We'd go all the way to Wickhambrook on our bikes,
Faith Bullock and me. And back. We'd go for miles.*

Joanie: *We all had bikes, didn't we? The Council supplied
me and Molly with ours.*

Molly: *That's right. Both at the same time. Brand-new ones.*

Joanie: *I remember going to collect them, and cleaning them.*

Molly: *Dad used to love cleaning a bike, didn't he? Out
on the flagstone, remember? He used Brasso.*

Jean: *He'd clean our shoes too, for Sunday school. It used
to be lovely and warm where his hand had been.*

His lips pursed in concentration, Olli moistened the wadded
duster from his tin of Brasso. Then he massaged it into the
iron curve of the handlebars, as was his way. His lightness of

hand and graceful motion belied the labourer's lot which fate had dealt him. Through the open door of the house, the familiar amalgam of old suet, musty armchairs and burnt cooking merged with Brasso's harsh, metallic scent.

Olli stood back and studied the rims of the bicycle and its gleaming spokes. He basked a moment longer in the bright sunshine. Then he turned to the door. It was time to visit mother and child.

Molly: *There was always kids being born at The Row.*

Doreen: *Yes, just think: Mum gave birth to every one of us in that little bedroom.*

Jean: *That's true! Eleven of us! It's amazing, when you think about it. She was so small! Can you imagine her giving birth to all us kids?*

The door had never rested true on its hinges, so Olli was unable to smother its noisy grating. For a moment, he stood very still, listening. Then he eased his way up the creaking stairs, to be met by the old nausea of baby's urine and the fusty, lime-washed walls of the bedroom.

Robbed of the shriek and clamour of the children, the house seemed deserted to him, and alien.

Jean: *We used to be farmed out to other families, didn't we, when Mum was giving birth? I went to Mrs Bullock's for ten days when you were born, Molly.*

Molly: *'Cos you was friends with Faith Bullock.*

Jean: *That's right. And, oh, how I loved it! I loved Mr Bullock smoking his pipe. I used to stand beside him, imitating his way of leaning on the fence, with one foot on it. He'd be watching for rabbits, with a stick in his hand. And I'd try and imitate him, sucking that pipe, with a bit of straw in my mouth.*

Jean and Faith were with Mr Bullock the morning he caught the rabbit. They both saw the sudden curving whip of his arm and the hurled, spinning stick find its goal. And both caught the victim's tiny yelp of death.

The two of them were at Mrs Bullock's table when she served the rabbit stew and mint. Their wonderful fragrance blended with the scent of pipe tobacco and Mrs Bullock's plums and the strange sweet aroma of her homemade rag mats.

And later, beneath an evening sky wide with golden summer, Jean and Faith took out their bikes and cycled together to the lake.

Jean: *It was lovely! Oh, I loved being with the Bullocks. I wouldn't have minded Mum having babies all the time!*

Molly: *Seems to me there was always somebody having babies at The Row! They sterilised Mrs Brown in the end – that's what I heard – 'cos she was just having babies. I reckon there was a lot of mischief went on there.*

Joanie: *Goings-on, you mean?*

Molly: *Yes. All them families packed together. And with Dad being away in the war. And them times he had to cycle to Essex to get work, and the men sleeping rough …*

Joanie: *You mean Mum had a fling while Dad was away?*

Molly: *Ask no questions, you'll be told no lies. But, I mean, just look at us sisters. We're all different from each other, when you think about it. I mean, don't it make you wonder?*

Doreen: *Oh, Mum didn't get up to any mischief. I'm sure of that. Not Mum. She was too prim and proper. As for Dad – well, Dad never had a chance to, did he?*

While Faith remained on her cycle beneath the trees, Jean dismounted and wandered to the edge of the lake. The air was tinged with the dusky warmth of hay, the still, brackish water and the murmur of summers wilted and gone.

Jean gathered up a handful of stones. Then, stooping, she hurled them, one by one, sent them skimming across the water to the clump of rushes on the far side.

Faith observed the flat, curving whip of the other girl's arm, watched the smooth, bouncing stones find their goal. For a few seconds, she stared in puzzlement, seeking some will-o'-the-wisp that had briefly danced before her, then fled.

Her lips pouted, Faith Bullock reached for the duster in her basket. With slow, graceful motion, she began polishing the silver handlebars of her bike, as was her way.

Sleuth

Jean: *He didn't dress at all badly, did he, the Reverend?*

Doreen: *Well, he was a tall man, very upright, not stooping or anything. So that was a good start, wasn't it?*

Jean: *He'd always wear that long black surplice, buttoned up to the top. So he cut an imposing figure.*

Doreen: *He was a strange one, though, the Reverend. Remember how he used to wander round the cemetery for hours, dressed in that surplice? He used to examine everything, didn't he? The trees, the church ditch, everything!*

Jean: *I had my first Woodbine in that church ditch. Hiding with John Bumpstead.*

Doreen: *Didn't he have a cushy old life, though? Cushy job, housekeeper, the Rectory to live in, all his books …*

He was first and foremost a man of the Scripture. But, privately, the Reverend was devoted, too, to the works of Conan Doyle. So, on the shelf beneath the timber beams of the reading room, *Early Bishoprics* and *Lives of the Apostles* rested in haphazard array with *A Case of Identity* and *The Adventure of the Cardboard Box*.

Sometimes, the appeal of the Great Detective could be discerned in the Reverend's Sunday sermons.

'Ye shall know the truth,' he would bleat to his congregants from the height of the three-decker pulpit, 'and the truth shall make you free. And when you have eliminated the impossible, whatever remains, however improbable, must be the truth.'

It was the cherry blossom time when the Reverend received news of his brother's passing. The funeral was a sorrowful affair but, armed with Godliness and his trove of detective lore, the Reverend found himself equal to his sad duty.

'Man is born of woman and hath but a short time to live,' he told the small party of mourners bowed at the grave, 'his days are as grass: as a flower of the field, so he flourisheth. For the wind passeth over it, and is gone, and the place thereof may know no more ...'

He lifted his eyes and studied the blossoming cherry tree at the Rectory gate.

'We may, of course, balance the probabilities and choose the most likely. It would be a capital mistake, though, to theorise before one has data. And circumstantial evidence is a very tricky thing.'

Motionless in her black knitted shawl, the widow surrendered to the flow of the speaker's words. Tugging gently at the wrists of her mittens, she, too, gazed quietly at the grey-timbered Rectory and its teeming cherry blossom.

She and her husband had known only a small tied cottage at the edge of the parish. Now he was gone, and its tenancy had expired with him. So it was no surprise that, soon – directly after the Reverend's next Sunday service, in fact – the widow was bold enough to enquire if he might be in need of a resident housekeeper. He bowed politely, said he would consider it and write to her.

Reflecting in the still of the reading room, the Reverend saw himself called by duties both Christian and familial. And at the same time, he saw the practical benefits that a woman's hand might bring to his sprawling home. He wrote:

> Dearest Mrs Matilda,
>
> I trust that you are bearing up after our great mutual loss. We may take solace in the knowledge that James is in the heavenly care of the Lord.
>
> Concerning your enquiry, I can say that I am indeed in search of a capable housekeeper. Would you honour me by dropping in at the Rectory that we may discuss details?
>
> In Christ's love,
>
> I am yours,
>
> W.M.

His eyes fell on his open copy of *The Adventure of the Dancing Man*. He thought for a while, then added:

> P.S. In a case of this nature, it is the details which are infinitely the most important.

Within the week, Mistress Matilda's small belongings had been transferred to her new station. The arrangement proved to be an amicable one. Her ham and tomato sauce savoury was most pleasing to the Reverend. And her smoothing iron made a fine job of the ecclesiastical garments. Mistress Matilda kept herself to herself and never disturbed her employer at his work.

In any case, the Reverend, like his detective hero, was a keen out-of-doors man. He would pace about his cemetery in the dawn light, stirred by the words of the Baker Street sleuth: 'There can be no question, my dear Watson, of the value of exercise before breakfast'.

At eight o'clock every Thursday morning, he would see his housekeeper emerge in her black shawl to tend the grave of the man to whom they had both been related. She would clear moss and twigs from the plot and brush its carved stone. Then she would place a small vase of flowers – hyacinths, perhaps, or chrysanthemums – and stand for a minute in a silent ritual of remembrance.

At this point, Mistress Matilda would look up, observe the Reverend, nod to him and smile. Then, tugging at her mittens, she would tiptoe back to the Rectory and resume her work.

During his reconnoitres, the Reverend liked to imagine himself in the role of the ascetic detective. He did not seek footprints or giant hounds, nor work on any case of tobacco-poisoning or abduction. Rather, the Reverend's quest for clues had a spiritual and charitable bent.

Gangly in his long surplice, he would stoop over the weathered mound of old Edwin Last. Inspecting it, the Reverend would convince himself that Edwin had edged closer to the church moat since last week. He took this gentle migration as uplifting evidence that the dead man was still nobly striving to hold a place among those dear to him, even as his bones mouldered beneath the nettles and chickweed.

Then the Reverend would study the graves of William and Harriet Rowe. For three-quarters of a century, they had lain side by side in the shadow of the south wall, which had been built from the ancient stones and flints of the field. Their mottled slabs had always gently inclined towards one other. But now, with each passing week, the observant Reverend convinced himself that the angle of lean was steeper than before. That God's laws of weight and gravity played their part in this, he well knew. At the same time, the stronger tilt renewed the Reverend's faith in humankind. It meant that William's and Harriet's loving union reached far beyond the grave and thrived still in their more blessed sphere.

One stormy night, a branch of the old yew tree was split in two, and the Reverend's eyes saw at once what others' did not. The fingers of the divided branch now pointed straight at the graves of a former gamekeeper and the poacher who had been his notorious enemy. This, too, the Rector took as an inspirational sign that the pair, adversaries in life, had found mutual forgiveness and unity in death.

One Thursday in August, a strange thing happened. The Reverend saw Mistress Matilda stooping at her husband's grave, brushing away its debris and paying her silent respects as usual. Then she cast him her customary nod and smile, wrapped her shawl about her, tugged at her mittens and left.

But when the Reverend approached the grave himself, he found no chrysanthemums or hyacinths – just daisies. Ordinary daisies of the field, and in a cloudy jam jar.

'It is, of course, a trifle' – the words of the Great Detective circled in his mind – 'but there is nothing so important as trifles.'

The next Thursday proved odder still. His housekeeper appeared at her dead husband's plot not wearing her black shawl. Then, after spending no more than a half a minute there, she nodded to the Reverend, smiled and left.

Inspecting, he found the carved lettering on the epitaph still clogged with soil from the night's wind and rain. No attentive widowly hand had reached to cleanse them.

The Reverend remained circumspect. 'Insensibly one begins to twist facts to suit theories, instead of theories to suit facts.' He took the measure of the Great Detective's calm judgement. 'It is of the highest importance in the art of detection to be able to recognise, out of a number of facts, which are incidental and which vital.'

Patiently, he awaited the Thursday to come. This time, the widow conveyed her customary nod and smile. Then she turned away immediately, leaving no flowers at all, nor any token of remembrance.

The Reverend's eyes rested on the grassy plot for a long time.

'A grave with no flowers is commonplace,' mused the interior voice of his mentor, 'and there is nothing so unnatural as the commonplace.'

Then again ...

'One important thing has happened, and that is that nothing has happened.'

Then he fell to counting the number of months since his dear brother had departed. Very slowly, his trundling mind analysed and ground the evidence as skilfully as any London sleuth.

It was the cherry blossom time again. Bending in his stiff buttoned surplice, the Reverend brushed the fallen petals from his brother's grave. Having gathered the twigs and loose moss into a bundle, he straightened and studied his handiwork. Then he turned and loped into the Rectory. As he passed the kitchen, he was met by the uplifting scent of ham and tomato sauce savoury.

The Reverend bowed courteously to Mistress Matilda as he entered the reading room. From the leather comfort of her chair, she nodded and smiled.

'Shall we continue, ma'am?'

She nodded again. Settling at his desk, the Reverend reached for *The Adventure of the Copper Beeches*, searched for his place and began to read:

'It is my belief, Watson, founded upon my experience, that the lowest and vilest alleys of London do not present a more dreadful record of sin than does the smiling and beautiful countryside.'

Mistress Matilda gazed out at the white blossoms of the cherry tree as the Reverend's bleat resonated about the rafters. Then, with hands deft and dainty, she peeled off her mittens and laid them on the polished oak desk beside her.

The Pirate

Molly: *That Sunday school outing to the seaside! Blimey, it was like going to Timbuktu!*

Joanie: *I used to be sick waiting for that outing. I looked forward to it so much!*

The trundling motor coach. The allure of the flat horizon. Creeping into view, the first escarpments. Bladders agitated with excitement.

'There it is!' 'Look!' 'Where?!' 'There! Look!'

The sea! And all the people, bobbing on the brown sand.

'Now, everybody out and stand beside the bus!'

Oh, I do like to be beside the seaside …

The pitiful mewing of the gulls. Waves' glorious crash and drag on tens of thousands of pebbles. Odour of old rope, dead fish and the salt-stained breeze. Pier, bandstand, esplanade.

'Now, remember: we meet here at four o'clock! When the big hand is on the twelve and the little hand is on the four! Susan Parr, what did I just say? ...'

I do like to stroll upon the prom, prom, prom
Where the brass bands play: tiddley-om-pom-pom!

Molly: *We weren't allowed to go in the water, though, in case we drowned. So we'd tuck our dresses into our knickers for paddling. In our Sunday dresses, mind you – calf-length!*

Joanie: *Ah, but we weren't all water babies, though. I mean, I wasn't keen on paddling, I can tell you that.*

Molly: *Well, brother Jack wasn't, was he? He hated the water.*

Joanie: *Oh, Jack. He'd just wander off by himself round the arcades. But, oh, it was all so lovely! I just wished the day would never end.*

Jack peered into the cavernous entrance and saw the beckoning tentacles of the octopus. 'Gems of the Seven Seas. Admission 3d.' Jousting with temptation, he counted his coins for the hundredth time. That would leave sevenpence – enough for a packet of whelks at the pier and perhaps a bottle of lemonade. Jack surrendered and bought his ticket.

Inside the cave wobbled a seahorse of papier-mâché. Its fishy hands pumped the tinny chords of 'A Life On the Ocean Wave' from a red concertina. Creaking and heaving on the swell of a painted sea was a miniature galleon, the skull-and-crossbones grinning from its mainsail. A bulbous whale loafed in a lagoon, spouting a chain of silvery bubbles. 'Having a whale of a time!' declared the yellow letters on its sailorboy hat.

His eyes dancing, Jack reached for the bubbles and tried to catch them. But they weaved and swirled away, to hide in the cave's shadowy roof.

A hook-fisted pirate in a red coat stood by a treasure chest, an open dagger thrust in his belt. 'The Scourge of the Sea': the words hung in rivulets of blood on a splintered plank above him.

Suddenly, Jack's throat tightened and his heart raced. Those heavy-lidded eyes, the black scar ... he recognised the pirate!

> Molly: *Do you remember the old man who used to sit in the allotment at the end of the village? He'd just sit and stare, in an old black coat ...*

> Joanie: *He always had his hand in his pocket.*

> Molly: *He did! As if he was hiding something. We were too afraid to go near him, weren't we? Well, I was. He really used to scare me, I can tell you. It was 'cos of his eyes and that scar on his cheek.*

> Joanie: *I heard he got that fighting the Hun. But Mum said it was from brawling. Sure as eggs is eggs, she'd say. Do you remember she used to say that? Sure as eggs is eggs.*

Jack gazed, paralysed, at the red buccaneer with the crooked scar and malevolent eyes. For it was only yesterday that Jack had stolen blackcurrants from the old man's allotment. And, straight away, the man had emerged from his shed, witness to the barefaced theft. Instinctively, and in panic, Jack had fled, throwing aside his stolen spoils.

Now, as he stood mesmerised by the evil eye before him, Jack's imagination played tricks. The pirate – the old man's murderous incarnation – had sworn to wreak vengeance on Jack the Thief. The glistening hook was going to drag him into the waves and pin him, thrashing, to the bottom of the sea, till he was drowned dead. Or he would be waylaid in the village: a seafarer's hulk would leap from the bushes by the school path and flash the deadly hook into Jack's heart. Or, biding his time, the pirate would seek out his victim in the black of the night ...

Jack's mind flailed in terror. He pictured the steel point ripping into his chest, imagined pain more torturous than the leather strap of his father, saw blood billow over his legs and shoes.

Frantically, he grasped at straws. He would run away, take to the woods, hide in a cave. But what if the pirate sought him out? Found him, helpless and alone and not a scream to be heard, nor any witness to the glint of the plunging hook ...

Suddenly, the pennies slipped from Jack's clammy hand and bounced over the flagstones. The proprietor – a pimply-faced young man – looked up from his window.

'Chuck it over 'ere, mate!'

But Jack didn't listen. For, as he scrabbled in the half-light for the coins, a desperate plan was taking root ...

'The little hand on the four ...' A tally of heads; reluctant, heavy-hearted departure; doleful eyes on fading sands as the coach hauled its way inland. But Jack was oblivious to it all. Haunted by the spectre of the pirate and with 'Ocean Wave' jangling in his head, he sat hunched at the back of the coach, darting glances left and right, watchful for the sudden glint of a silver hook.

In bed, he strove to keep his eyes open and alert. But, time and again, a red-tinted phantom crept to his side, seeking the boy who had stolen blackcurrants. 'Fee, fie, fo, fum, I smell the blood of an Englishman ...'

In the morning, febrile and exhausted, Jack set out on the mission of despair he had resolved to undertake. As he approached the allotment, the sight of the stolen blackcurrants, scattered and crushed at the side of the lane, fired a weakening shock to his legs.

The old man was there, in his customary place, one hand in the pocket of his coat. A rusty bucket stood beside him. Jack's heart hammered as he halted at the gate, held by the man's sardonic stare. Had he actually been waiting for Thieving Jack, the blackbird with two legs?

Quaking, Jack pushed the gate open and shuffled forward on legs almost too weak to bear him. The man's mocking gaze did not leave the boy's face.

Jack held out his hands. The brawling scar throbbed as the man squinted at the thing Jack was holding. Slowly, he lifted a gnarled claw and took the boy's offering.

It was a stick of pink seaside rock. Price: sevenpence.

Petrified, Jack awaited the outcome of his act of appeasement. Swept by the breeze, his legs no longer seemed to be his own.

For a long minute, one hand still in his black coat, the man studied the propitiatory gift. Then, nodding, he thrust it under his belt, like the pirate's open dagger. Fixing his eyes on the boy again, he slowly drew out his hidden hand.

Jack's heart lurched as the vision of the hook leapt to his mind.

But the old man had pulled out a thin metal tube, with a handle. It was no bigger than the stick of rock. His eyes still on the boy, the man bent and dipped the thing into the bucket beside him. Lifting it out, wet and dripping, he gently pumped the handle.

Into the summer air danced a surge of silvery bubbles, weaving, glistening, alive. The man watched Jack's amazed face as they swayed and cascaded in the morning sun. Then he dipped the pump into the soapy bucket again, and launched another dancing mirage.

His face alight, Jack met the old man's ironic eyes. Then he lifted his hands and tried to catch the shimmering trail of bubbles. Some swayed flirtatiously, and hovered, inviting capture. But the rest sailed up and away, up and away, over the wide land and across the seven seas.

Mulled Wine

Joanie: *I'd be sick with excitement, waiting for Christmas. I'd wake up in the night and go down to peep at that stocking under the tree! I couldn't help myself!*

Molly: *Oh, you was always getting up with everyone else still abed, Joanie. You was a right little worryguts!*

Joanie: *I know! I couldn't help it! Do you remember the Christmas when Mum brought that doll into the house? Well, I knew it'd be there, down in that front room. And it scared me stiff, with those eyes. But I still had to get up early and go down to peep at that Christmas stocking, even with that doll staring at me!*

Jean: *That hobgoblin! She gave me the creeps too, that thing.*

Doreen: *Her eyes used to move, didn't they? They sort of rolled when you tilted her left or right. I'd never seen anything like that.*

Molly: *Sometimes, she really seemed to be watching you and thinking, what mischief can I get up to here?*

It was right after Aunt Rosie's funeral that Mum found the lady hobgoblin. Rummaging in her dead sister's chest of drawers, she was amazed to discover the clothy, grinning thing. The blue corduroy jacket was threadbare and the knitted bonnet had lost its old gleam. But she was still in one piece, the hobgoblin. So Mum brought her home: a remembrance of the girlhood she and her sister Rosie had shared in the long-ago.

Oh, there were no lady hobgoblins, of course. Everybody knew that. But in *The Fairyland Gift Book*, the two sisters had a picture of a plump little fellow falling into a cauldron, his face wrenched in terror. 'The Hobgoblin Falls to His Doom': so read the fearsome caption. And the mischief-maker's bulbous head and eyes were the spit and image of the girls' own lumpy doll. So Lady Hobgoblin they named her.

Doreen: *Mum brought her home and perched her on the coal scuttle, didn't she? In the front room.*

Molly: *That front room! Why ever didn't we have it made into a bedroom? It was never used, except for funerals and Christmas night.*

Christmas night …!

Squeezed together on the horsehair sofa, the children bubbled with excitement. The puck-faced doll grinned at them from her coal-scuttle pedestal. Without her customary starched apron, Mum cut a less sombre figure, and a less shrewish one. Like a priestess on her throne, she sat gazing at the unique sight of Dad on his knees at the grate.

He thrust a burning spill into the kindling. Then he got to his feet and pressed an open newspaper against the wall, covering the open fireplace, forcing the flames to draw into life.

Molly: *I could have watched Dad all night, drawing up a blaze.*

Jean: *It was really dangerous, the way he did it, when you think about it.*

Molly: *Oh, it used to fascinate me. 'Cos I loved a good blaze!*

The rare luxury of the front room. The dance of the fire and the frolicking shadows. Heady largesse of oranges, walnuts, pink and white sugar mice with string tails. And mulled wine!

Mum had concocted it with the bottle of port she'd saved from Aunt Rosie's funeral. The children clamoured to wrap their palms round the steaming pot, then screwed up their faces at its cloying scent.

'Think of your Aunt Rosie …'

Dutifully, they hauled up the memory of the dead woman's bony face and fragile limbs. And they wondered again if Tommy Nunn would be sent to Hell for saying, once, that she looked like a scarecrow.

Broken nutshells, smoke and burning coals, the exotic odour of orange, hot sugar and nutmeg – all conspired to banish the room's fusty staleness. The swelling flames caught the gleam of the silver locket at Mum's neck, and sought out the hobgoblin's elfin smile and the glint of her tin buttons.

Suddenly, Dad was on his feet again. He plucked the doll from her dais and dropped her on the carpet. Then, gripping the tongs, he fetched a slice of coal from the scuttle and dumped it flat on the fire. A squeal of dismay met the brief quelling of the flames. But as they licked around the shard of coal, they soon found new life, and threw fresh gambolling shadows about the little room.

Mum got to her feet to gather the children's orange peels in a jam jar, for stewing. Then, bending, she righted the doll on her coal scuttle and lightly brushed the blue jacket. Her long minute of indignity over, the creature glared at the company in silent disgust.

A tranquil lull settled as they gazed into the flames.

It was Mum who broke the silence. In a still, subdued voice – almost not Mum's at all – she began to talk of her dead sister. Of a long-ago time before the children could remember, when Aunt Rosie had been wedded. Of the husband who was taken early, and not another man in the village to woo her, not after the dreadful war, and Aunt Rosie never one to flaunt herself. And of the aid and comfort the lonely woman had received from the village, not least from Mum herself.

Fingering her locket, she paused. Then:

'And your father played his part.'

She sipped at her wine and did not lift her eyes from the lapping flames. The children peered up at Dad, a heavy brooding bird, the contours of his head softened in the luminous glow.

Mum's hypnotic voice resumed. Dad had cycled all the way to Aunt Rosie's, she said, whenever a strong hand was needed. He had mended Aunt Rosie's chicken run and raised her potatoes. And it was Dad who had heaved the copper pot from the bottom of Aunt Rosie's well when the chain broke.

Mum paused again. This time, she turned her eyes on her husband. With an unsteady hand, he refilled his cup, spilling red drops as he did so. The slanting gaze of the hobgoblin noted every sway and motion.

Her voice a floating trance, Mum then told the children of the seafaring grandfather they had never known. When he was home from the sea, she and Rosie would sit with him in the dusk of the evening, the hobgoblin too. And in the stillness, he would tell them of Faraway: of fish that flew, and the weeping long-tailed parakeet, and of crimson hills and lakes of gold painted in the sky.

And he taught them songs. Songs to sing aboard a vessel on a becalmed sea, songs to stave off madness, songs which no one knew but the three of them, and the hobgoblin.

In the flickering shadows, the children's eyes, big as mirrors, turned from their mother to the ancient doll in her grey bonnet. She grinned back at them, still, sardonic, inert.

And Mum told the children of the lookout their grandfather had made – a crow's nest, in the language of the mariner. Built in the yew tree it was, a bower of timber planks, with bound branches for walls. From the masthead of their silent ship, Mum and Rosie could hold vigil when their father was gone a-voyaging. And, on their imaginary looking-glass sea with no swells or motion, they would sing the songs they had learned at his feet.

After he was dead and gone, the songs belonged to Mum and Rosie, and to the vigilant hobgoblin. The tryst remained theirs, to share and to hold. And now, God rest her, Rosie was gone, her earthly toil ended.

The haunting tale done, Mum paused and sat motionless before the smouldering coals. From her high perch, the doll watched with sharp, capricious eyes.

Then, slowly, gently, Mum slid into a lilting chant. It was a hymn of sadness, drenched in a waveless ocean mirroring the wide vault of the sky. Wordlessly she crooned, her shoulders swaying and her fingers clutching the locket at her throat. Before her, the flames rose, fell, strove to rise again, then settled to a quiescent sea of red. The children glanced sideways at the illumined face of their mother, a sentinel atop her crow's nest again, gazing at a wide and stagnant ocean.

Then, an amazing thing …

At first, Mum did not hear the plaintive chant that had joined her own. Then she ceased her crooning and stared at her husband.

Molly: *Dad singing! We'd never heard him sing!*

Jean: *Never! Not till that moment. It was right strange!*

Doreen: *It was like a dream.*

His eyes and lips closed to the world, Dad swayed forward and back, forward and back, humming his wife's yearning tune. Then, slowly, gently, words clothed his melancholic drone:

> Said a fair-haired swain to his true love:
> 'Let us sail to the tropic land,
> Find ease of heart by the mangrove
> And silver in the sand.'

In the throb of the shadows, Mum's hooded eyes fixed on her husband. His face thick and ponderous, his hands wrapped around the cup of wine, he sang on:

> Said the lady to the fair-haired swain:
> 'I'd sail to the end of the seas
> For a love that's true, silver or none,
> And a precious heart to please.'

As the slow, cracked words faltered to their end, silence fell.

Molly: *He wasn't used to wine, was he? He was a beer drinker, was Dad.*

Jean: *Too true. That mulled wine, it was too much for him. It made a sentimental old fool of him.*

Molly: *I mean to say: Dad singing! He must have drunk practically the whole bottle that night.*

The hobgoblin watched Dad attentively as his eyes opened. The first thing he saw was the red spillage on his trousers. Frowning, he brushed at it. Then he looked about him in bleary puzzlement. Suddenly, he emitted a loud yawn. Doreen, at his side, caught it instantly, embellishing hers with a tiny squeak. Young Jack was next, and around the circle sailed the yawn, followed by the gimlet eye of the hobgoblin.

Then, abruptly, without a word, Dad lurched to his feet and hauled himself drunkenly to bed.

Only Mum had not yawned. Impassive, she sat gazing at the fire in the iron grate. Around her, young eyelids sagged and fell, Doreen uttered her squeaky yawn again, and, all of a sudden, Christmas was done.

Something of magic it had, that night of mulled wine and weaving shadows, of walnuts and sugar mice, and the mesmeric tale of the oceans, the strange, grieving song of their father and, through it all, the hobgoblin's button eyes and half-crazy grin.

Mum laid the children in their bed, to curl their toes around oven-warmed bricks. Then, alone, she padded carefully down the stairs, and back to the silent front room. There, atop her precarious mast, waited the hobgoblin, her face clenched and wary.

It was Joanie, rising early next morning, who saw the bulbous charred shape among the embers, and an edge of blue corduroy.

Joanie: *Burnt up, she was. Burnt right through.*

Molly: *I wish I'd seen how it happened. I loved a good fire!*

Joanie: *Burnt to a cinder, she was.*

The children whispered their suspicions. But not one of them felt inclined to question their mother. For the whole of the long, wrought day, she flung herself into a frenzy of work and banished every vestige of peace from the home. Combative in her starched apron, she clattered crockery, scrubbed pans, washed and shovelled, slammed doors and windows, and hounded the children from one place to another with her shrewish bark.

As for Dad, he cut a grim and dismal figure, trudging off to his labour in the dark, and then, when the day was done, sitting drooped over his supper with barely a word to say for himself.

So the girls could not be sure if the sharp-eyed mischief-maker had fallen to her doom. But she was gone, that much they knew: gone the way of every tryst and promise.

Then, children being children, they forgot the lady hobgoblin. And her name was never spoken in the house again.

And neither, for a very long time, was Aunt Rosie's.

Albert Last

Jean: *Some families had it hard, really hard. It was bad enough for us, with Dad being so fond of his drink. But I mean, some families just lived from hand to mouth. There weren't enough work …*

Doreen: *Not on the land. Not year-round.*

Jean: *I mean, take Albert Last …*

Joanie: *Oh, he was a sad case, was Albert. Really sad. He used to be carried home, didn't he?*

Jean: *Carried home to his wife. And she was a battleaxe. She was a real shrew, that Ruth Last. She led him a life.*

Joanie: *Oh, it was a sad business altogether, with Albert. It was the war that did it …*

Eyes gleaming in his blackened face, one hand outstretched, the coalman cut an oddly theatrical figure.

> Here's a health to the King and a lasting peace,
> To faction an end, to wealth increase ...

Sturdily erect in the Pump Room of The Six Bells, the man gave richly of his full-chested baritone.

> Come let us drink it while we have breath,
> For there's no drinking after death ...

The singer raised his palms dramatically and stretched out his next line:

> And h-e-e that will this health den-y-y ...

Then, his teeth bright, he pumped both powerful arms to carry the men into their grand chorus:

> Down among the dead men, down among the
> dead men,
> Down, down, down, down,
> Down among the dead men, let him lie!

As Jim Wheeler watched the swaying and chanting, his mind drifted back to boyhood afternoons in the old barn. The bittersweet detritus of straw. Wrestling. Conkers. Mad, raucous games of bat and ball. Swinging from the black rope on the high beam, one foot in its noose, and screeching like monkeys.

And singing ...

They used to sing old music hall songs, shoulder to shoulder, up on the hayloft. 'Daisy, Daisy'. 'Where did you get that hat?' 'Two Lovely Black Eyes' ... Jim remembered Lenny Cracknell's flat wail; the bold, carefree ring of the Howlett brothers, who had perished side by side with the Second Battalion; little Percy Brown's easy choirboy grace; and the crooning bleat of Albert Last. They would still be weaving their songs long after darkness had settled on the rickety barn ...

In the Pump Room, the coalman's bold baritone was thrusting forth again:

> While smiling plenty crowns our board,
> We'll sing the joys that both afford ...

The men sat on the edge of their bench, alert, eager for their cue.

> And the-e-ey that won't with us comply-y-y ...

At the beating of the coalman's stubby arms, the chorus gave throat again:

> Down among the dead men, down among the
> dead men,
> Down, down, down, down
> Down among the dead men, let him lie!

The coalman slumped back in his seat, panting, his grimy hands dumped before him on the table. He had given his all.

A wave of friendly raillery followed.

'Come on, boy, you carry on!'

'Ain't givin' up now, are you?'

'Just gittin' in my stride, I was!'

'Won't be askin' you again, boy!'

Smiling weakly, teeth a-gleam, the man shook his sooty face. Still grumbling good-naturedly, the others turned and took up their gossip again. Before long, though, they drifted to the subject of grain prices and wages, and their talk became edged with worry. Word had got around that Len Cracknell was giving up. With so little land under plough, farming had made a poor man of Len, and an exhausted one.

Beneath lowered eyelids, Jim Wheeler glanced over at Albert Last. Perched, bird-like, apart from the others, Albert had gaped at the singing men with his curiously big eyes. Jim thought of Albert's bullying shrew, and another child on the way, and bleak seasons to come. There'd be no smiling plenty for Albert. Not now, not with Len Cracknell gone. For Len had striven more than anyone to put work in Albert's way. And who else was going to hire a man who sank to his knees at the sight of a darkening cloud?

> Molly: *They'd go out searching for Albert Last, remember? And they'd find him laying in the fields …*
>
> Doreen: *And his tools scattered all around.*
>
> Molly: *It was the war that did it. That's what they said.*

The remnants of the Second Battalion were reticent men, and talked little of what they had seen and shared. And never once did Albert speak of his demons. Everybody knew of them, though, and greeted Albert at every turn with the balm of kindness.

But still, in the gathering of the dusk, the silent, playful creatures would reach and sink their metal claws into Albert's brain. Then rats crawled in dead men's eyes. Hooded crows, stooped at their carrion, flapped monstrous, torn wings. And Albert would hear again the iron howl of the cannons, see black swathes of smoke spew across the sky.

Then the doomed chorus would take up their chanting in grim harmony with the guns. And the grinning demons would press Albert, crush him, helpless and sobbing, down, down, down, down in the flinted soil, there to let him lie. Then, all their jesting done, they would fold their jagged claws and sleep.

Jim looked up. It was the coalman again. His eyes flashing, he was on his feet again, pounding the table with a black palm.

'Give a man enough rope, he'll hang hisself …!'

The men were arguing loudly now. It was about a landowner in the next county who had ordered a newfangled machine from Canada. To replace paid labour, it was said.

Jim half listened to their agitated gabble. Then, looking about him, he saw Albert's empty seat. He had not seen the man leave. But now, suddenly …

'Give a man enough rope …'

The coalman's words lapped against the walls of Jim's mind.

Gathering up his hat and coat, his chest tight with fear, he hurried from The Six Bells.

In the dusky half-light, the slatted door of the barn hung open. Peering in, his forehead pulsing, Jim Wheeler caught the old remembered staleness.

And, to his relief, he saw Albert. The man was up on the hayloft, his tense, wiry form held in a shaft of moonlight. The old rope was hanging directly in front of him, its noose heavy and iron-black.

Laboriously, Jim heaved himself up the creaking ladder. Then he took a place at the other man's side and stared down. Matted straw and rotting wooden planks lay scattered in the murk. He recognised the rusty tin bath which had served as a wicket in the long-ago games of bat and ball.

In the thickening gloom, Albert did not take his wide, gaping eyes from the rope. Oppressed by its proximity and the weight of silence, Jim shifted uneasily. He sensed a stirring in the other man, fancied he heard the bustling scurry of a rat …

Where - did - you - get - that - hat?

Jim turned and stared at the black profile of the man beside him. Then, wrenched to the challenge, he countered the old familiar words with his own funereal growl:

Where - did - you - get - that - tile …?

Side by side, the two men continued their bizarre incantation, each blending with the other's sawing monotone:

> Isn't it a nobby one?
> And what a proper style ...

Under the echoing rafters of the empty barn, the two friends droned in grotesque concord. Swaying together, they picked their way through the slow dirge:

> I should like to have one
> Just the same as that.
> Where'er I go, they shout 'Hulloa,
> Where did you get that hat?' ...

They were still at their chanting, Jim Wheeler and Albert Last, long after night had filled the old barn, and demons slept.

Empire Day

Jean: *I can see Mum now, scrubbing away in that washhouse, with her bar of Sunlight.*

Joanie: *And those wet days when the washing wasn't dry, so it would have to be hung in the house, and there wasn't time to get a proper meal.*

Doreen: *Sometimes, it all seemed just too much for her, you know what I mean?*

Joanie: *Poor old Mum. The life she had! Dad was no good to her whatsoever, him boozing all the time.*

Joanie: *And money always short. I don't know how she managed – poor old soul. She was always low. No wonder she gave up sometimes, poor old thing.*

Jean: *Used to give up completely, didn't she?*

Joanie: *Well, she had depression, I reckon. She got so unhappy and miserable. She wouldn't comb her hair. It just used to hang there. Remember how she would sit in that chair for days on end? She wouldn't do her hair and she cried. She'd look so bedraggled, with her long hair. I reckon she had a bit of a nervous breakdown.*

Joanie: *She used to look so worn out sometimes, and the jerries would need emptying.*

Doreen: *Well, Dad, he'd drink so much down at the pub that he'd fill those things right up! He was no use to man nor beast, was Dad.*

It had been a rush for Maud, getting an early dinner on the table, then harrying the children into readiness. With the mounting excitement, Joanie had acquired her usual headache. So she had been bundled upstairs to mind the baby. The other children – Jean, Doreen and young Jack – were already on their way, so Maud was now hastening to make herself presentable for the occasion.

Her husband slouched by the door in his starched collar, with the droop of a beaten dog. Usually at this hour, he'd have been at his ease in The Six Bells. Maud eyed him wearily as she struggled with the locket at the throat of her blouse.

With a spurt of dread, she felt an old fatigue settling on her.

An unfamiliar sight in her vast black frock, Mrs Savage hustled around, handing tiny Union Jacks to the parents. Buzzing expectantly, they sat on tablecloths spread over the buttercups and bull daisies of the village green.

Maud nodded bright greetings left and right. Then, unwillingly, her eyes were drawn to the closed curtains of the Palfrey house on the edge of the green. Quickly lowering her face, she took out her tablecloth and spread it at her feet.

Beside her, Olli gazed at the wooden mast before them, and the white tapers fluttering from its neck. Then, screwing up his face, he tried to recognise the children clustered under the oak tree. All held tiny Union Jacks and wore red-white-and-blue paper hats. More homemade flags were strung along the boughs of the ancient tree.

There was a deal of scuffling and prodding till the children were quelled by a sharp adult bark. Then, smiling graciously, Mrs Savage turned to her audience.

The rituals of May 24 – Empire Day – had begun ...

'Age shall not weary them, nor the years condemn ... Ye Mariners of England that guard our native seas ... Wider still and wider ...' One by one, each boy stepped forward to recite his memorised chunk of patriotic verse, then to receive kindly, supportive applause '... For frantic boast and foolish word ... Drake, he's in his hammock ... Lord of our far-flung battle line ...' Mrs Savage, a watchful black raven, stood beating time with her flag '... Dirty British coaster with a soot-caked smoke stack ...'

Young Jack, hips swinging, delivered his slice of Masefield in the mincing singsong that infuriated his sisters. Tight-lipped and anxious, Maud glanced about her. But she needn't have worried. A good-hearted surge of applause met her son's homage to the imperial dream.

Then came Wilfie Brown ...

Wilf, all elbows and bones, took his stance and glared at the faces before him. They gazed back and waited while he searched for his opening line.

The waiting continued ...

A muscle pulsed in Wilf's jaw and he wrung his tiny banner with white-knuckled force. But he did not speak. The pause lengthened, punctuated by gently prodding nods and smiles. Still Wilf stood rooted in petrified silence.

Suddenly, his mouth fell open and loosed a screeching wail. At the same instant, he shot a hand under his crotch, turned and tried to run. Howling strongly and striving, one-handed, to stem the drops seeping through his fingers, Wilf made again for the haven of the oak tree. A heavy shape lumbered forward – it was Mrs Brown – and, instantly, the long-rehearsed salute to King and Empire was in ruins.

For no one – not parents nor *dramatis personae* – had the stomach to continue. Why? Because Wilf's strange, desolate howl had wrenched at every heart. With terrible crucifying truth, it had pulled drab-faced mothers and haunted men to the edge of an abyss, and forced them to stare into its depth. Wilf's grieving wail had given voice to lives of drudgery in squalid, crowded homes. It had spoken of bad teeth and ulcerous legs, of joyless, cavernous nights and unwanted births, conceived in drunkenness. And of the dread, stretched across the years, of destitution and of the bailiff's knock, and the clang of the workhouse door. They threw away the key once you were in the workhouse. And stuffed you up the chimney when you were dead. 'Rattle his bones over the stones, he's only a pauper who nobody owns ...'

On the green, children, cowed and subdued, crept into the arms of their mothers, and thought of the silent ghosts who dealt out sickness and stole lives. And they remembered the Palfrey girls, Grace and Annie, who would not be seen again, never no more. And eyes flitted across to the curtains of Mrs Palfrey's house, and she never showing her face since the day, and her husband, once a praying man, given now to grief, and to drink.

Mrs Brown's wide bulk straddled the gnarled roots of the tree as she cradled the sobbing Wilf. Gradually, though, his convulsions began to subside to a whimper. At the same time, a chain of tiny, random events began to unfold. Someone daintily blew her nose – could it have been little Mrs Lane, the postmistress? Another person coughed. Then a flight of gulls, traversing the sky, decided to pause and hover. The air took on new and gentler sway, and roused the buttercups. The branches of the oak tree lost their static droop, and grass shimmered in the quickened breeze.

A throbbing could be heard, faint at first, then firmer and stronger. Heads turned. And there was the thin, stooped figure of the Rector, trundling a handcart up the road, bearing large cardboard boxes tied with string. Mrs Parker of the village shop was there too, weighty and dogged, labouring behind him.

As the cart was rolled onto the green, parents and children respectfully climbed to their feet. The Rector, agitated, tried to nod and smile to everyone at once. Rigid in his long black surplice, he fumbled helplessly with the knotted string. Mrs Parker's clawing hands assisted the dithering reverend fingers and, finally, the wonderful treasure was revealed.

Buns, with sugar icing! Bottles of lemonade, and glasses!

'Right, smallest at the front! That's you, Mary Potter …!'

With schoolmatronly force, Mrs Savage herded her charges into line. From the back, ecstatic faces strained to glimpse the amazing largesse, Wilfie Brown's among them. He craned his neck, ogling with red-rimmed eyes.

Sticky buns were crammed into eager mouths, each child saving the iced top till the end. As they gorged and slurped, the sonorous words of the Rector's catechism drifted on the warm breeze: '… Christian duty … colonise and serve … less happy lands … noble task …'

Then:

'Mr Sayers, if you please?'

Mr Sayers, the portly garage owner, had been waiting quietly beside a wicker chair covered by a linen cloth. Now, with ceremonial care, he lifted the cloth to reveal a gramophone. Deeply conscious of his standing as sole mechanic of the village, Mr Sayers gave the gaping metal horn a studious polish. Then, with regal calm and shirtcuffs patched with sweat, he began to turn the handle.

And the old ritual began.

Weaving and swerving, cotton-smocked girls circled the mast in twos and threes, interlacing ribbons as they joined and rejoined the flow. Smiling in the sun, parents clapped their hands to the surge and sweep of the ancient dance. Olli stood behind Maud, enfolding her while they eased their hips and swayed to the rhythm. As the stubby shape of Doreen jigged its mazy circle, she caught their eyes and waved. But Jean, mosquito-light, all nimble grace, lived only for the force of the dance.

The lingering last chords; a long-held wave of applause; a commotion of bright-eyed chatter – '... did enjoy that ... like the olden days ... always loved a maypole ... right graceful ... credit to all ... wonderful sight ...' Then a folding of tablecloths; a slow brushing-down of frocks and best trousers; a flurry of smiles and leave-taking.

'Them girls o' yours look right lovely, Maud!'

'You done them a treat, that you 'ave!'

Her eyes shining, Maud bobbed a curtsey of thanks. In blushing confusion, she took off her hat and dabbed the sides of her hair. Then she pressed against the curve of her husband's arm. Running a finger beneath the press of his collar, he eyed the horizon.

'Rain tonight, Maud.'

She walked at his side, demure, smiling, her eyes lowered. Jean and Doreen straggled behind, knotting daisy chains and boisterously chanting the maypole song.

Olli glanced down at his wife and offered his arm. She took it lightly, shyly, young again.

Joanie: *Didn't Mum look nice when she was dolled up? Her hat all prettied up with flowers.*

Jean: *Mum always managed to have us turn out clean and presentable. Poor as we were, and all us kids.*

Doreen: *We didn't have a lot, as a family, did we? But we were really happy. It was lovely, playing in those great fields, in the bull daisies. You don't get 'em now, a field full of bull daisies.*

The Thatcher

Doreen: *He wasn't all there, was he, the thatcher? He wasn't right in the head. Remember how he used to stare at things?*

Jean: *As if he was trying to remember something.*

Joanie: *Well, he'd fallen off a ladder once, poor man. So they said.*

Jean: *That was at the Lotbinieres' place. He fell on his head. That's what I heard. So no wonder he wasn't all there.*

Doreen: *He repaired our roof once, Jean. Do you remember that? You and me were there. Do you remember?*

The thatcher leaned his ladder against the wall, and gripped the sides, testing its firmness. Then, hauling a bundle of rushes over his shoulder, he ponderously climbed to the roof. Grasping the beams with both hands, he laid hard into the slope and peered up at the moon's bright circle. Cautiously, still holding fast, he began to place his rushes over the last of the worn thatch.

> Doreen: *Mum hated thatch, didn't she? She was convinced it was going to catch fire one day. She always wanted slate, did Mum.*
>
> Jean: *It was Dad who ordered thatch.*
>
> Joanie: *'Cos thatch lasted, didn't it? That's what they used to say.*

Suddenly, shrill laughter burst out below him. Clinging with both hands, the thatcher looked down. Two girls, about twelve and thirteen, were bent over the rain butt, shrieking and batting the water with their open palms. Then, abruptly, the older girl tired of the sport and wandered off. The other scurried after, drying her hands on her grubby pinafore.

The thatcher's bulbous eyes were still gaping at the water in the butt long after it had resettled. Not till a sharp breeze broke his trance was he stirred to take up his work again. Then, with firm, probing fingers, he continued laying out the dusty sheaves.

Cautiously, he climbed down to fetch his willows for binding the rushes to the beams. Standing beside his handcart, he rubbed his knees and stared at the ground.

A plate of cold meat and potatoes and a mug of tea rested on the table. But the thatcher's slack gaze was held by the moth which lurched and banged at the window. His hands gripped his thighs as the creature battered its wings and its black body in frenetic despair.

From her place in the scullery, the woman of the house watched him in puzzled silence. Suddenly, her husband clattered into the room, back from his inspection of the roof.

'That better last, boy, the money I'm payin' you!'

His manner was surly, querulous. Oh, he knew thatching was a hard living, in wind and weather, and cruel to the bones, and a man could end up with a broken neck. And worse. Oh, yes, he'd heard all about the accident at the Lotbinieres' place. But, as loath as the next man to part with a shilling, he cut a truculent figure as he fished out his purse.

'Last you ten years, squire' – cowed and timorous, the thatcher did not meet the other man's eyes – 'a fair ten years, Lord be willin'.'

From the scullery, the woman clucked her tongue as she watched the coins being counted into the thatcher's hand.

Shards of cloud scudded across the moon's white face as he mounted the ladder again and straddled the ridgeline of the roof with his thighs. Then he fixed to it a shape he had crafted from willow sticks and rushes. It was the upright figure of a sword – the thatcher's signature, to mark the work as his own.

> Jean: *That little sword was up there for years, pointing straight at the sky.*

> Doreen: *It was still up there when they pulled the house down – what? – twenty years later.*

Standing beside his handcart, the thatcher rubbed his knees pensively. Then, bending, he wrapped his tools into oilskin and laid them in the cart. Looking up, he caught the hard silhouette of the willow sword against the moon's clean light. His brow creased in puzzlement, he continued staring for a long minute.

His reverie was interrupted by muffled giggling. It was the girls again. They were in the doorway now, one behind the other, watching him. When he met the older girl's eyes, she stepped forward, impudent and grinning.

'What's your name, mister?'

Jean: *But he never said a word, did he? He just stared at us. Like he was trying to remember his name.*

Doreen: *I don't reckon he could remember it. I don't reckon anybody knew his name. He was just the thatcher, wasn't he?*

Jagged clouds rampaged across the sky as the thatcher passed the markers which guided him on his homeward path: a barred gate; the contours of a dead oak; an iron cattle pen. As he trundled down the dirt track, the crevices in his face deepened as he tried to gather the images drifting loose in his mind: a sword; the moon; a white cascade …

It was as he was approaching Blunston's pond that the clouds suddenly dispersed. The moon broke out with fresh, brilliant force and the thatcher caught its reflection in the pond. His memory leapt. In a blazing instant, he caught the swirling, errant pieces and bound them together. And the thatcher saw himself, a boy again, at a gleaming lake, kneeling above his own reflection. He was brandishing a toy sword, its blade silhouetted hard against the glaring moon. And the thatcher heard again the long-ago song of the summer grass.

He fell to his knees. Reaching into the water, he scattered the moon's reflection into silvery dance, and stared as its shimmering pieces met and blended in their old array.

Then, rapidly, the malignant clouds gathered again, obliterated the moon and swept its light from the land. Desperately, frantically, a moth beating against the pane, the thatcher strove to hold the old sweet joy and to bind it in his brittle mind.

For a long time, his bulging eyes stared at the darkened water. Then, lost and baffled, he gave up. Slowly, he climbed to his feet again and rubbed his knees. Then, reaching for the handrails of his cart, the thatcher peered down the narrow path and trudged into the night.

Harvest

Jean: *The pinnie ladies, we called them. They'd stand in their gardens at Pheasant Row, all day. In their white pinnies, just staring at the world.*

Doreen: *Just watching anything that happened.*

In their starched pinafores, the two women presented a bizarre contrast. Mrs Boreham was thin and sharp-nosed with dark, hidden eyes, as if wary of the light. Mrs Sturgeon, a straggly hulk of a woman, had rabbit teeth and bulbous lips which hung slack and open.

Doreen: *They used to win prizes for their cakes at the Flower Show, the pinnie ladies.*

Joanie: *Oh, the Flower Show! That was lovely! I was so excited when I went, I was nearly sick!*

Jean: *It was a highlight in our lives, the Flower Show.*

Doreen: *It was. It was.*

Jean: *There was your wild flowers, and your cakes and loaves and sponges. There was your knitting, and your sewing and needlework …*

Joanie: *And the men brought their fruit and vegetables.*

Doreen: *You were a good knitter, Jean. So was Joanie.*

Jean: *And the Rayner girl, Ellie, she'd always get prizes for her loaves.*

Ellie was serving at the tea stall when she noticed the newcomer. She was tall and angular, and moved quietly among the trestle tables, with their sticks of rhubarb and red-ripe onions. From the woman's riding coat and boots, Ellie supposed that she was the new guest at the Blunston farm where Ellie did kitchen and cleaning.

The Rector pressed his fingertips together and peered at them: '… excellent entries … extremely high standard … terribly difficult to judge …'

As Ellie curtsied and took her prize, she again caught the woman's eye, attentive and alert. Her face lowered and flushing at the ripple of applause, Ellie returned to her duties at the tea stall.

Five minutes later, she looked up.

'I would love to know your secret.'

The woman's speech was weighted and even, as if rehearsed. Her thin eyebrows hinted at irony. Ellie, red-faced and confused, did not reply.

'You do have a secret?' A pause, then: 'I mean, how do you make such bread? So firm and shining.'

Ellie caught the woman's clean scent of lavender, and observed the nut-brown of her skin. Horsewoman's skin.

Ellie still could not find words to shape a reply, but the woman went on:

'You might show me one day.' She gazed placidly at the green gauze of the table, smoothing it with her fingers. Then, she moved away, smiling lightly, as if the whole thing had been a joke.

At night, the woman's odd contralto resounded in Ellie's mind – 'you do have a secret?' – and she could not cast off the image of her slim grey skirt and riding crop. And of her own hands, kneading and pressing the dough, yeasty-fresh, down and away, down and away, gathering, turning, smoothing, rolling, and every surface greased and warmed to golden brown.

> Doreen: *She was Farmer Blunston's sister, wasn't she, the visitor? She came to the farm right soon after Mr Blunston lost his wife.*
>
> Jean: *He was getting on in years, Mr Blunston. It was just as well his sister came that summer. Well, that's what people said. She came to help him get along, like.*
>
> Doreen: *She was very well dressed wasn't she? I reckon she had private means.*
>
> Jean: *Oh, I think the whole family did. Must have. I mean, Farmer Blunston kept his horses, didn't he? And his wife used to have all her dresses made in town.*

Playing Samaritan to her widowed brother, the visitor won the esteem of many villagers. But not the pinnie ladies. As she rode down the street in the morning, her shaped chin and the cut of her riding clothes met their raking gaze, and lit a flame of resentment. Dark, suspicious eyes sank deeper in their sockets and sagging lips pouted.

* * *

One day, soon after her arrival, the visitor appeared in the farmhouse kitchen.

'Good morning,' she said.

Ellie bobbed a small curtsey of greeting – 'Mornin', ma'am' – and continued her kneading at the table. The heels of her hands pressed, deep and firm, into the fleshy dough.

The woman wore a green sack-like dress, its neck and sleeves intricate with oriental patterns. The odour of lavender brushed Ellie's senses. Inclining her head, the woman smiled.

'So, you'll be revealing your secret one day?'

'Expect so, ma'am.'

The woman ran her fingers over the edge of the table. She was close enough for Ellie to observe the thin lines in the bronze skin of her face. Suddenly, without a word, the woman turned and glided from the room.

Ellie stood very still, her hands flat on the table, her cheeks aflame.

Next morning, as she approached the farmhouse, Ellie saw the fresh ruts where Farmer Blunston's cart had left for the village. She did not look up at the windows. But she knew she was being watched.

In the kitchen, instead of reaching for her utensils, she stood. And she waited.

Soon she heard a light scraping on the flagstones, caught the haunt of nut-brown skin, and the waft of lavender. Ellie did not turn her head.

She took a late path across the dusky, teeming fields and made her way home up the deserted lane. But the sentinels of Pheasant Row saw what they saw, and surmised what they did not.

Soon, measured pauses and slanted looks were being exchanged in quiet places. And before long, in the glow of oil lamps in village cottages, oblique innuendo acquired the substance of gossip.

Such goings-on! They were beyond the laws of God and nature, wagging tongues asserted. And beyond the limits of what good Christian folk could condone. Something had to be done.

Live and let live, whispered others. There had been suffering and loss enough, God knew, and more to come. So let comfort be sought, in whatever way or guise.

The two vigilantes of Pheasant Row wasted no breath on their husbands. For they knew that the men held fast to a notion, evolved and affirmed in The Six Bells, that some business was for womenfolk alone. So, fired by righteous verve, the pinnie ladies sought out the Rector instead.

Pale and distressed, he studied the joining of his fingertips.

'God moves in mysterious ways,' he bleated, 'they passeth all understanding ...'

The women gave up on him instantly.

'A word with you, Mr Blunston? If you please?'

It was not the first occasion the good farmer had been waylaid by the pinnie ladies. This time, he was walking Dollie and Depper, his retired workhorses, down the back lane to the farmhouse. Nodding courteously, he lent only half an ear to the women's venomous whispers. For he had long shared his late wife's view that they were addle-headed busybodies.

But, later, when he climbed to the loft to fetch for the horses, he stared, perplexed, at the shape of the hay at his feet. Easing his way down the ladder, he gave fresh thought to his interview with the two ladies.

Grim-faced, Farmer Blunston stood in the barn for a long time, gazing at his boots.

The air was thick with dusty chaff and straw. Men in corduroys and kerchieves passed cans of tea, then continued loading the heavy sheaves. Horses strained against the creaking weight of the wagons.

In the farmhouse, the woman was not to be seen. But Farmer Blunston was there. He called Ellie into the parlour.

'I'm needin' extra hands on the fields, Ellie.' At the sudden clang of the threshing machine, he paused and glanced through the open window. 'So you'd better speak to Mr Jermaine first thing, and help with the sheavin'.'

Ellie, her mouth tight, curtseyed and turned to go.

'So I don't want to see you here at the house, Ellie. Not till harvestin's done. I'll pass you the word. You understand?'

'Yes, sir,' she said.

The machine hummed on, pouring its streams of golden grain into the sacks.

Doreen: *Wasn't it lovely when the corn was being harvested?*

Joanie: *Do you remember when the rabbits were trapped in the last of the corn? They'd go round and round, right frantic.*

Doreen: *And then they'd make a mad dash for it. All at once. And we'd catch 'em.*

Joanie: *We knocked 'em on the head.*

Doreen: *And we chased one into Blunston's wood, didn't we, Jean? Remember that? You and me, with sticks.*

Jean: *That's right. It was slower than the others. I reckon it'd got stunned by the machine. It was just hopping along, with little pauses.*

Doreen: *Like it was stopping to think.*

Jean: *Then we got lost in Blunston's wood. And saw Ellie Rayner.*

Doreen: *We did. We did. She was in a sort of clearing, wasn't she? She was sitting very still on a fallen tree. And hoofprints all around her.*

Jean: *Hoofprints everywhere.*

Doreen: *We didn't stay, though, did we? Not after Ellie glared at us. We just turned and ran!*

It was on the Sunday of the harvest festival that the woman abruptly left the village. Perhaps Farmer Blunston had had his fill of sisterly aid. Or there were matters elsewhere which required her attention.

At Pheasant Row, curtains parted and inquisitive eyes watched the woman's departure.

But they did not see her carriage halt at the village church. Nor did they see her climb out, her arms full.

Fingertips conjoined, the Rector nervously greeted each arrival at the church door. Soon, though, it became evident that there was some disruption in the House of God. His brow palpitating, he left his post and ventured inside.

Around him everywhere were the gaudy columns of harvest flowers: chrysanthemums, larkspur, lilies, sweet Williams, sunflowers. Piled at the altar lay swathes of wheat, wooden boxes teeming with fruit, apples, carrots, and fat marrows on tufted carpets of corn stucks.

Then the Rector saw the cause of the turmoil: two large loaves had been caught by the rays of the sun filtering through the stained window.

At that moment, Mrs Sturgeon and Mrs Boreham entered. They, too, stared at the bulbous loaves, dumbfounded. Behind them, more villagers filed in, and added to the dissonant uproar.

For each of the loaves had been kneaded and pried into silent, eerie expression. One bore the comical face of a witch, its pointed chin and hook nose crowned by lizard eyes in pits of crusty brown. The other, a pale flat mass, had slack, bulging lips and vast buck teeth. In the dappled light, they rested, drawing wave upon wave of croaking laughter.

Then Ellie Rayner entered the church. She heard the rich, good-natured sound rising and doubling, like yeasty dough in the warmth of the sun. It climbed the walls, greased the surface of the columns and the stained windows and beams, filled the ancient place and swelled to the highest rafters of the nave. Ellie closed her eyes and sank in the soft, gold-brown harvest of the laughter.

Tutankhamen

Molly: *Remember Dad's remedy for a cold? A bottle of stout! He used to take the rake from the fire and plunge it into the stout. And that was for us kids!*

Joanie: *Ah, there were some rum old cures in those days. It's a miracle we all survived.*

Molly: *Hot onion for earache …*

Doreen: *Clove for a toothache!*

Jean: *Well, whenever we got stomach ache, Mum used to send us to bed with a hot brick …*

Doreen: *Wrapped in newspaper. I remember that. It did the trick too.*

Joanie: *And what about Dad with his ulcers? He had terrible ulcers, did Dad. And he swore by his Rennies tablets. But, really and truly, there was no cure for ulcers.*

Not then. Some things there just wasn't any cure for. I mean, think of TB.

Doreen: *And diphtheria. Sister Gladys had diphtheria, didn't she? She got sent to the Isolation Hospital – ooh, for months.*

Jean: *It was a real scourge, diphtheria.*

Doreen: *It was. And scarlet fever. Remember scarlet fever? …*

Her tomboy energy suddenly spent, the girl crept indoors and drooped onto the sofa. Soon, a headache came on and she was quickly put to bed by her mother, a thin-shouldered widow with perpetually troubled eyes.

At his customary seat in The Six Bells, the girl's uncle drew a black, corroded object from his pocket and passed it around.

'Found it next to a rabbit hole,' he said. 'Now what do you reckon to that?'

Handing the thing one to another, the men studied it, frowning.

'Well, don't you go throwing that away, George,' said one, passing it on. 'Seven years' bad luck, you'll get, throwing away a ring.'

'Do you get yourself wedded with that, George,' said another, winking at the man beside him. 'That ring's an omen, my boy. Reckon you'll be wanting someone, to skin them rabbits of yours!'

Everyone laughed, for George was well liked at The Bells. He was a fair dealer, and never pressed a man for a price. He raised his eyebrows in mock caution.

'A whistling woman, a crowing hen …'

'Ain't neither fit for God nor men!' the others chanted, and they all fell to laughing again.

George, smiling, dropped the crusted object back in his pocket.

*   *   *

By late afternoon, the girl had the chills and her throat was swollen. Reading danger, her mother got her up to the attic, and hung a curtain across the door. She instructed the boys not to linger on the staircase, and to hold their breath as they passed.

George was distraught at the news of his niece's illness. He promptly left his rabbit-catching devices and hurried to the house. Bending, he examined the red bumps clustered about the girl's neck. Motionless under the dark, sloping roof of the attic, she lay on her side and did not speak.

George stood helpless, gripping the book he had brought, and fingering the ring in his pocket. Miserably, he gazed across at his sister.

'What's to be done, Faith?' he whispered hoarsely.

Her jaw set, the woman did not lift her eyes from the girl.

'We tend and pray, George. We tend and pray.'

He placed the book at the girl's bedside – *The Story of Tutankhamen*, it was called – and peered again at the tiny red bumps.

In the morning, he was there again. The bumps had spread and 'strawberry tongue' had appeared too, with its telltale white coating. George stared in distress at the girl, while her mother moved around the tiny room, busy with disinfectant.

When they had gone, the girl, turning listlessly, laid her hand on *The Story of Tutankhamen* and half-opened her eyes.

Carefully, George hung a brace of rabbits on the farmer's gate, completing his part of the bargain. Then he trudged to The Six Bells, the remaining rabbits dangling from the handlebars of his bicycle. There was no chafing that evening, and the bartering was done quietly, for the men had heard of his niece's sickness. Subdued and apart, George took his ale and fingered the crusted ring in his pocket.

*   *   *

In her delirium, the girl stared vacantly at the pictures: Tutankhamen's gold mask, his caskets and treasure rings, his thin-wheeled handcart and gilded bed.

As George draped his trousers over his brass bedstead, the black ring fell and rolled across the floor. Mindful of the seven unlucky years, he bent, picked it up and put it back in his pocket.

All the lights of Cairo had gone out when Tutankhamen's tomb was opened, so the book said. And wings of death had beaten over the Englishmen who excavated it. Their dogs howled and died and their canaries were swallowed by cobras. Such was the power of the pharaoh's curse.

Suddenly, during the girl's febrile browsing, a gust came from nowhere and blew out the candle at her bedside.

In the morning, George stood for a long time, staring in dismay at the girl's flushed forehead and cheeks and her pale mouth. In agitation, he plucked at the black ring in his pocket.

Time, place and sense swirled in the girl's restless fantasy. She imagined a warrior king entombed in the earth of the village. His battle spoils lay in the shadows, strewn beneath the sloping roof of his burial chamber. At the foot of the king's bed, threaded with gold, lay his sword and shield, and his heap of treasure rings. As he bent over them, probing and searching, his brows creased and his grisly lips moved to the sounds of an ancient curse.

The girl was torn from her twilight world by a scream. It was her younger brother, downstairs. The old cat had leapt and clung to the door latch to let herself in, as she always had. But this time, when the boy opened the door, the hanging cat, its paws still holding fast, was dead.

Later in the morning, old Tottie Heddon almost perished. Mad Tottie was found in her nightdress, crawling down the street on her hands and knees, wailing fit to die.

Then there was Lainston's scarecrow, a rotted skeleton of wood and twine. It had stood since men were boys, they said. And now there it lay, flattened, and the yellow beads of its eyes plucked out.

Then Jack Dawes had tumbled into the pond, backside first, on his way home from The Bells. In head-shaking bewilderment, men asked however such a thing had come to pass. For old Jack had trodden that path for twenty years, and never once took harm, till now.

Next morning, when the boys tiptoed their fearful way down the staircase, gripping lighted candles in jam jars, the sandpaper rash had spread silently over the girl's body.

George was on his knees in Lainston's field when he heard the strange sound above him. A flapping, a beating of wings … He looked up, but saw nothing. So he bent again to his task, thrusting the ash stick into the hole, in search of grey rabbit hair.

He met with a blockage: collapsed earth, perhaps, or a stubborn root. Frowning, he pulled out the stick and examined it. The tip was too thin for scouring. An abrasive edge was needed. Fumbling in his pocket, his fingers lighted on the ring.

He rammed it around the point of the stick – a good fit – and set about his scouring again.

When George pulled out the stick, the ring was gone: sunk in the village soil whence it had come.

Raising her face, the girl's mother mouthed a prayer of thanks, then she carried away the half-eaten bowl of rabbit stew. George lingered a while longer, peering at the girl's faded rash, and at the first of the peeling skin. Then, nodding to himself, he left too.

*   *   *

In her exhausted dream, the girl saw the warrior king stir and rise. She watched as he crept about his chilled, dank tomb beneath the village. He paused and stooped over his captured caskets and treasures, and his shield and studded sword. Then, his rheumy face set and frowning, he made a careful tally of all his sacred rings.

Nodding to himself and fingering his beard, the king returned to his gilded bed, to sleep for seven years.

Molly Miss

Jean: *Mum'd get that riled when she knew we'd been out flirting. She hated us being out with boys.*

Doreen: *In case one of us brought home trouble!*

Joanie: *I used to think she meant trouble with the neighbours. Or stealing.*

Doreen: *I had no idea what she meant! Nobody explained anything to us!*

Joanie: *Well, Mum never did. I used to think babies grew in the cabbages!*

'Hussies!'

Mother spat the venomous syllables across the table. Tales had been told, so she knew of her daughters' antics down at the river.

'Brazen hussies! I know how you'll end up! With your boys and your lipstick and your flaunting! I know how you'll end up! Sure as eggs is eggs! You'll bring trouble back here! I know!'

From her shadowy refuge at the foot of the stairs, young Molly watched as her older sisters bowed beneath the storm of the tirade. But Mother didn't know that Molly had been at the river too.

Oh, she was too wary ever to venture to the water's edge, was Molly. Safer for her, the hedgerow of vines, where she could enfold herself. There, her fancy could take flight, and she could peer across the river at the cottage where the painter lady lived, and watch the smoking chimney paint grey shapes in the air.

From her haven of trailing vines, Molly had seen the Banham boys lolling on the bank and heard their low murmur meet the tranquil lapping of the river. And she had seen the heavy shape of Edie Collins lumber towards them, her basket on her arm.

'Smell ...' Edie had dangled her straggling posy of dandelions before the brothers' faces 'Go on, smell. You won't be sorry.'

The boys had stared at Edie and at each other, grinning. Then:

> Sissy in the morning, can't catch a flea!
> Sissy in the evening, can't catch me!

Hearing the taunting chant across the river, the boys suddenly had no eyes for dismal Edie. They had leapt to their feet, pranced over the thin ribbon of water and, whooping fiercely, given chase to Jean, Doreen and Joanie.

Then, from her citadel of vines, Molly had seen Edie's shoulders slump, and her eyes turn to beads, like Aunt Nelly's pig when it was being goaded by the old dog. And she had watched Edie shamble away, the heads of her futile, ragged flowers drooping at the edge of her basket.

* * *

A few days later, Molly was sent to run an errand to the cottage. The family's dressmaker neighbour pressed a brown-paper parcel into her hands.

'Compliments of Miss Flack,' she wagged a gnarled finger in the girl's face 'and these are the leggings ready and done. Now, what are you going to say?'

As she neared the cottage, Molly found that the vines were now swathed in a white foam of eglantine. She stopped and pressed herself in and cupped her palms around some of the blossoms. Careful not to damage the sweetbriar hips of the autumn to come, she peeled away the petals and inhaled their faint apple fragrance.

> Vine, vine and eglantine
> Clasp her window, trail and twine …

Then she saw the boy.

Bigger and older than herself, in the serge trousers and cloth cap of a farm boy, he was squatting down at the riverside, threading string onto a fishing pole. As he worked, his thin, bare forearms caught the yellow lightness of the sun.

Molly sensed he must have seen her as she was pressing the pink-edged blossoms to her face. Now, feigning to ignore him, she inhaled more of the feathery scent while he fixed worms to the end of his line. He glanced up at her once. Then, with a dabbing flick of the arm, he cast the line into the water.

A breeze stirred and shifted the light, pale treasure of eglantine around Molly. Thorns clutched at the sleeves of her dress, her hips and her arms. As she pulled them away, she watched the boy leaning to the water, playing his string line against the river's easy drift.

The cottage door was swept open by a galleon of a woman with an incongruously tiny paintbrush poised in her fingertips. Its bristles, Molly saw at once, bore the same crimson as the woman's gash of lipstick.

A dark eyebrow was raised in stern enquiry.

'And what might be *your* name, young lady?'

Molly had been silently rehearsing – 'Compliments of Miss Flack …' – but now the woman's imperious manner flustered her. The eyebrow arched higher.

'Molly, miss,' she blurted.

The woman bent and plucked the parcel from her fingers – 'Then follow me, Molly Miss!' – and strode indoors. Clambering after her, Molly abruptly found her senses thrown into turmoil.

On the wall before her were painted a tall Grenadier Guardsman, scarlet and erect, and, beside him, a cadaverous vagabond in stripes of pink and yellow. Molly recognised at once the colours of soap: Lifebuoy, pink and soft, for washing yourself, and Sunlight, yellow and hard, for clothes. Preening alongside the two figures was a gold-tinted pelican, its gawky feet curled on a seawave of jagged green. Above it swirled a painted blaze of comets, moons and planets.

'For you, Molly Miss,' – cake and lemonade had magically appeared on the table – 'and don't take it into your head to run away. We've more work for our lady seamstress!'

Her brain spinning, Molly groped for words of thanks, but too late. The woman was gone. Turning to the wall, Molly stared again at the amazing painted trio of soldier, wayfarer and bird.

'Flaunted herself!' Bent in wrathful arc, Mother hurled her bitter words across the table. 'That wretched Collins girl! Flaunted herself! Cavorted with boys, and flirted, and butter wouldn't melt in her mouth! And now look! Our fine Lady Collins has gone and brought home trouble!'

From her staircase refuge, Molly saw the livid creases writhe in her mother's face and thought of the corrugated wrapping of the parcel she had carried that morning. Jean, Doreen and Joanie gaped at each other around the table.

'And that's what's going to happen to you, my fine ladies! You mark my words! You'll bring home trouble, just like that Collins girl. And when you do – when you do – there'll be no place for you here! Don't you dare think you can bring trouble back here! You'll find that door locked and barred!'

She ceased her harangue to watch Doreen crumple into clenched, silent weeping.

'Mark my words! You bring home trouble, and there'll be no place for you here!'

Frowning at the black beams above her rickety cot, Molly heard the churning of the iron key as Dad locked up for the night. Then she peered into the murk to seek out her sisters in their shared bed and to study the fall and rise of their breathing.

They were there. All three. All alive and safe. The vast black door had been locked downstairs and none of them had brought trouble or been barred from home. They were safe. So …

> Wash your hands and wash your feet.
> Now it's time to fall asleep.

But Molly did not sleep. Instead, the picture of Edie swayed in her mind. Molly saw the heavy-limbed, cumbersome girl, her lumpy sleeves ruffled in the wind at the bank of the river. And she pictured Edie's moon face and her plump fists gripping the basket that she had brought home filled with trouble.

Like vines in the breeze, the images of a tumultuous day turned and stirred in Molly's mind. And her quicksilver fancy seized them and wove a tale: a fantastical, liberating, night-coloured tale, to banish trouble and repaint the world anew.

In her tale, Edie found a new home. It was a riverside cottage, clothed in eglantine, where three companions stood sentry, to forestall trouble. The upright Grenadier, in tunic, bearskin and bandoliers, flanked his raggedy pink-and-yellow friend and the gilded, swollen-breasted bird, sharp of beak and claw. And down the bank of the river stood the boy to take Edie's basket from her hands. A hitch of his leather belt, a flick of his bare arms, and he cast the dark cargo into the ambling river. Side by side, beneath the dancing moon and the stars, Edie and the boy watched the last of trouble drift away.

Doreen: *We never saw her again, Edie. She had to leave the village, didn't she?*

Joanie: *It was one of the farm workers got her into trouble. That's what I heard.*

Jean: *And she wasn't at all pretty, was she, Edie Collins?*

Next afternoon found Molly again among her vines, inhaling the faint, brittle perfume. 'Vine, vine and eglantine ...'

She waited till she saw the boy arrive at the river bank. As he looked up, gaping at her, she reached out her hands. Puzzled, he held his distance. Then he stabbed his rod into the muddy soil of the bank and, hitching at his belt, slouched up the slope towards her. Behind him, the river tugged gently at the string line.

The boy entered Molly's white labyrinth and, immediately, the rabble of hooks and thorns clutched at his clothing. He batted them with short swipes of his open hands. But, stubbornly, they clung to his serge trousers and gripped his rolled sleeves.

'Smell ...' Molly raised her handfuls of petals to his face. 'Go on, smell. You won't be sorry.'

Flesh and Blood

Jean: *Remember the golden rule? Eat pork only in a month with an 'r' in it.*

Doreen: *Never from May to August. That was the rule.*

Joanie: *'Cos it was hard to keep meat fresh in those days, wasn't it? Before refrigeration.*

Doreen: *Mum used to keep ours in a metal box. Remember that box? With the mesh?*

Jean: *But Uncle Darkie, he'd always bring fresh-cut meat.*

Doreen: *We were lucky, weren't we? Uncle Darkie being a butcher.*

It was true. For Uncle Darkie had no match in the arts of scalding and severing, removing head and trotters, cooling, cutting, carving, boning and rubbing salt into shoulders, bacon sides, loins and chops. Following the flash of his blade and the spurting of the hot blood, Uncle Darkie could conjure up a black pudding fit to shine on the table of King George.

> Jean: *We always had a mixed grill those Sundays Uncle Darkie and Aunt Elsie came. They always brought some liver with them.*

> Joanie: *That's 'cos a butcher was allowed to keep the liver for himself, after the cutting and boning. That's what Dad said.*

During the week, the jangling two-wheeled wagon was used for hauling carcasses, ham hocks and pork belly. But on Sundays, Uncle Darkie mounted glass cases with tallow candles at the rear. Then Aunt Elsie could fancy she was in a pony and trap during her stately ride across the village.

Behind them, on the wooden slats, would rest their posy of violets or daisies and Uncle Darkie's trimmed liver, wrapped in brown paper.

> Doreen: *Remember how Mum used to stretch the lining of the pig's stomach over the meat? The lace curtain, we used to call it.*

> Joanie: *It used to get all crispy, didn't it? It was lovely, the lace curtain!*

> Jean: *These days, you couldn't get it, 'cos of health and safety.*

Aunt Elsie and Uncle Darkie would pause at the churchyard, and lay their small posy beneath the yew tree. Then, the quiet ritual done, they would climb back into the wagon and trundle on their gentle, winding path.

> Doreen: *We always had a nice spread when Uncle Darkie and Aunt Elsie came. Jelly and custard …*

> Jean: *We weren't allowed to sit up at the table, though. Not till they were gone. We had to sit side by side on the settee.*

Doreen: *Except you, Joanie. You used to hide under the table.*

Joanie: *Well, I was afraid of Uncle Darkie, wasn't I? I was afraid of those dark features of his.*

Doreen: *Oh, he was nice, Uncle Darkie. He brought a pig's bladder once, inflated. For brother Jack to play football with.*

But Uncle Darkie counted as an 'interloper' among the villagers. It was largely because of his sombre colouring. 'Painted with the tarbrush' was what Dad had to say about it. But, besides that, Uncle Darkie was a town man. To folk shaped by the brooding drag of the seasons, his quick speech and the jaunty angle of his cap suggested slyness. Too clever by half, he was. That's what some people said. Oh, men would greet him courteously enough if he had a mind to visit The Six Bells. But no one shifted on a bench to make way for him, or asked what weather he thought was in store, or enfolded him in the banter that moved in the tavern's smoky air.

Still, even Dad grudgingly owned that his sister had a found a good provider in Uncle Darkie. He cared for Aunt Elsie as only a loving man could, and gave his sturdy all to bring a gleam to her clouded eyes.

But what a forlorn creature she was, Aunt Elsie. She would sit clenched and still for hours, bringing nothing to the gabble and gossip of the family table. So how bewildering was that long-ago afternoon when …

> Ride a cock horse to Banbury Cross
> See a fine lady on a white horse …

The girls and young Jack frolicked and sang around Uncle Darkie's horse and cart. The flanks of the fretful animal trembled in the shafts of the wagon, and its chestnut head dipped and swayed. The voices blended in shrill harmony.

> Rings on her fingers, bells on her toes,
> She shall have music wherever …

Wide-eyed and still, the children ceased their sport and their chanting. They stared at the open door of the house. A curious yelping sound … Something was amiss. Cautiously, with the tallest, Jean, to the fore, they crept up to the door and peered inside.

Jean: *It was Aunt Elsie. Sat in Dad's rocking chair, she was …*

Joanie: *And her face buried in her hands.*

Jean: *A-pouring out her heart, she was. And never saying why.*

Joanie: *And Dad flapping round and round and blowing his nose. And Mum crying too …*

Doreen: *And holding Aunt Elsie in her arms …*

Jean: *Just pouring out her heart, she was. And never saying why.*

The little woman's tearful flood and the antics of their parents held the sisters mesmerised. But young Jack's gaze was fixed on the creased, stricken face of Uncle Darkie, and on Uncle Darkie's hooded eyes beneath the cloth cap. And Jack remembered the day of the abattoir.

He had never told his sisters about it, never breathed a word. They had heard so many of his fanciful tales that they wouldn't have believed him anyway. So the day of the abattoir was lodged in Jack's mind like a fantastic dream, private and unshared.

The squealing pigs, clamouring in stomach-turning stench, and pressing fleshy red nostrils against the mesh of the sty. Uncle Darkie at the abattoir door, searching for his key. Then with his lantern, flooding yellow brightness into the murk, beckoning Jack inside. The stone trough; the menacing silver hook on the rail; barrels; iron pots; the scrubbed table; knives, gleaming and heavy-handled; and Uncle Darkie's wide-bladed cleaver …

In the reeking demi-world of the slaughterhouse, Jack watched, spellbound, as his uncle lifted grey intestines from a metal bowl. His tanned face creased in concentration, the man drew them with slow, enormous power through a tightened fist, then dumped them, stripped and slobbering, into a bucket at his feet.

Then Jack saw the picture pinned on the door. It was a gaudy, flimsy thing, torn from a threepenny magazine. Seeing the boy peering at it, Uncle Darkie brought the lantern closer, so that its banner lettering could be read:

> Westward the Star of Empire Takes its Way
> Canada: the Right Land for the Right Man!

In the picture, a single bloated star cast its white beam over a horde of pigs corralled in fences. From the chimney of a green-roofed cottage curled a dainty wisp of smoke. The silver thread of a railway stretched across the background.

As Uncle Darkie closed the door behind them and locked it, the porcine cannibal screaming intensified. The din climbed still higher as he walked to the sty and spilled into it the eviscerated contents of the bucket.

Uncle Darkie took Jack to the washhouse, where hands and arms were scrubbed. Then they made their way to the horse and wagon waiting at the front of the house.

'We'll walk 'er, chum.' The man tugged his cap to a tighter angle, then carefully laid the posy of daisies and his wrapped liver in the back of the wagon. 'She did 'er work today. Never drive a good 'orse to death.'

The animal clop-clop-clopped its way forward, untroubled by the loose rattling of the slats and its jingling harness. A fragment of song roved through Jack's mind:

> '… rings on her fingers, bells on her toes,
> she shall have music wherever she goes …'

As Uncle Darkie walked beside the horse, he stroked its head and the thick chestnut skin of its neck.

When they stopped at the churchyard, Uncle Darkie made Jack stay on the wagon while he laid his posy on the tiny plot under the yew tree. On his return, he did not speak, but pulled chunks of bread and fat pork from a draw-string cloth bag and shared them with the boy. They perched side by side on the top of the wagon, chewing. Jack watched the slow working of Uncle Darkie's copper cheeks as he gazed at the churchyard. Then:

'We learned about Canada at school.'

Uncle Darkie's chewing stopped. He continued staring ahead.

'From Mrs Savage. We learned about Canada.'

Still his uncle said nothing.

'It's a land of – of opp – oppri –'

The boy fenced with the unfamiliar word.

'Opportunity.'

As he spoke, Uncle Darkie did not take his eyes from the churchyard.

Jack had been ready to describe the aniseed flatness that was Canada on the schoolroom map. But now, with Uncle Darkie so still …

Then:

'No good for your Aunt Elsie, chum.' He was still staring ahead. 'Not Canada. She wants 'ome.'

He turned his hooded eyes to the boy.

'Your Aunt Elsie, she can't leave 'er flesh 'n' blood.'

Jack stared at his uncle's brown-leather face, and wondered. Flesh and blood … Jack was sure he didn't mean the meat which he hacked and carved, or the gleaming black pudding. No, the boy knew that flesh and blood meant family: Mum and Dad, brother Bill, his sisters. And Jack himself. They were Aunt Elsie's flesh and blood.

He pictured the woman's set face and her taut, closed body. And he wondered which of the wide, jostling family she was unable to leave, which of them kept her from the green cottage in Canada and the sprawling herd under the white star. For, with a child's instinctive sureness, Jack knew that Aunt Elsie, submerged in her drab reverie, felt no real attachment to any of her family.

He sat and waited for Uncle Darkie to explain.

But Uncle Darkie did not speak.

That night, in the backyard, Jack stared up at the illumined vastness and tried to pick out the Star of Empire, moving on its westward way. To Canada.

Later, in bed, he dreamed of the hands of a celestial giant plunged into the wide firmament, squeezing its pinheads of light through an invisible fist, gathering them up, jingling them in palmfuls to the wafting of a song:

'... she shall have music wherever she goes ...'

A scream of panic tore the night. Behind the mesh, the beasts ceased their grunting, and gaped at the abattoir with terrified red eyes. Then they added their own wild bedlam, as if sharing a vision of their frantic, doomed cousin being hoisted on the rail.

As always, the victim's scream stopped abruptly, to be followed by the clatter of carving, heaving, chopping, hacking. This time, though, the butchery took on a strange, frenzied violence. Slowly, steadily, it mounted to a tumult of savage flailing that prompted the bestial howling to fresh heights of distress.

Then, suddenly, with a metallic crash, the din inside the abattoir ceased.

Through the thin walls, a fresh sound emerged, one which the beasts had never heard nor, given their transient lives, were they to hear again.

It was the sound of a man weeping, choking, grieving. And pouring out his heart, and never saying why.

The Urn

Doreen: *Most of our lot left the village, most of our generation. We did, didn't we?*

Jean: *Well, none of us wanted to be shipped out to service, to be chambermaids, like our older sisters. And Bill and Jack, they didn't want to be well-sinkers, like Dad.*

Doreen: *I remember, on my first night away, I laid down and cried my heart out. I'm glad I went, though. 'Cos there was no future for us in the village, was there?*

Jean: *Not when you think about it.*

Doreen: *But, we still thought of it as home, didn't we? I mean, even now. We'd all want to be laid to rest in the village, wouldn't we? I mean, that's where our roots are.*

Molly: *You speak for yourself, Dordie! As far as I'm concerned, you can roll me in a ditch when my time comes – just as long as I get a good send-off!*

The menfolk of The Six Bells looked up and ceased their quiet talk as the visitor entered. Then, courteously, they nodded to him, and resumed to their low murmur. But one of them, a solitary heap in the shadows, continued to stare. Glancing at the old man, the visitor fancied he recognised the mark of idiocy in his gaping manner.

He was shown to his room by candlelight. Stooping, the publican lit the oil lantern, then withdrew quietly, closing the door after him. The image of the publican's shrunken, peaked face hung in the visitor's mind as he gazed around at the straddling beams and uneven plaster walls. Then he opened the bare cupboard and peered into unlit corners, fancying he heard echoes, vibrations, restless spirits. Would the shades of his ancestors, he wondered, be visiting him here? But then, a practical man, he banished the foolish thought as soon as it arose.

He sat on the edge of the bed and, in the flickering glow, brought out the wrapped casket which contained the remains of his mother. He was about to place it on the shelf of the cupboard, when something led him to hesitate.

Puzzled, he gave the urn a shake, then another, more vigorous one. Then he glanced around him guiltily, as if witnesses might have caught his disrespectful act. He shook the thing again, more reverently this time.

There was no sound, no rustle of ashes. Surely an incinerated parent should offer an audible sign of having been reduced to particles? Or did fleshly remains re-solidify during years spent in an attic? Or perhaps, given time, they turned to gas? Or had the cremator packed them so tight as to allow no leeway for slippage or shift? Or had the maternal remnants expanded and lost density, so as to cling to the interior walls of the capsule?

Guilt struck him – a quick dagger to the heart – at being drawn down this path of thought. Quietly, he refolded the brown-paper wrapping around the urn and placed the thing on the cupboard shelf.

A lurid brown stain marked the only mirror in the room. The visitor studied his baggy jowls and the droop of his custard face. Then, despondent, he went to bed.

The dingy walls of the tavern gave cheerless comfort for his breakfast of weak tea and bread-and-jam. He peered out of the window: a muddy pathway, clumps of tangled nettles, a coppice of elms with sagging branches. And rain.

A sight of years had passed since his mother had asked to be taken home. Now, finally, a widowed man, he was about to perform his last filial duty and spread her ashes over her native earth. During the long time of postponement, he had gradually acquired a second, weaker motive for the journey – an obscure wish to tread the soil from which he himself had stemmed.

He was not disappointed at the greyness of the village. Indeed, he had expected it to be quiet and dull. He had anticipated, though, a miniature quality too, some degree of quaintness and charm. But the place was sprawling and drab. The sight of its mean, dismal windows and the ubiquitous drenched nettles cast over him a gloom to match the leaden sky. A fresh wave of despondency passed through him.

At the cemetery, the black rain battered the tin roof of the small three-sided shelter. Perched on its log bench, he hauled his mother out of the bag and unwrapped the brown paper. Straight away, he encountered an unthought-of difficulty: the urn was sealed. How was he going to prise her free?

The rain fell harder on the black engraved stones before him. He placed the obdurate vessel on the bench and sat thinking.

Then a new unforeseen problem arose. The idea of returning his mother's ashes to the earth that had bred and nurtured her had seemed a noble and worthy one. It was, after all, what she had asked for. But now that he was faced with the actual task, here in the village cemetery, where exactly …?

He looked around him. Surely not over the plots of other tenants. Nor could his mother possibly be strewn on the stubby, boot-scarred verge lining the pathway, to be trodden by hunch-backed mourners.

He had an idea. Since he couldn't break open the urn, why not just inter it whole? After all, this was what had been done to the countless boxed corpses before him. But, then, what tools did he have for digging and scouring?

Again, he felt a blade of guilt in thinking in this pragmatic way, but its edge was less keen now, and he could reflect how easily, how practically, he could ponder such questions. Had the sleeting country rain begun to flush away the emotional bond he had had with his mother? But then, what was he really doing but dumping a can of old soot on a patch of grass he had never seen?

And what had bred in him the ludicrous idea that he had some native connection to this place, this clutter of old houses and nettles and soaked fields?

He looked up sharply. It was the old man. He was holding an armful of glistening-wet kindling wood. Wheezing, he dumped himself beside the visitor and gazed out at the rain-drenched acres of the entombed. Then:

'You're Mary Pask's boy, aren't yer?'

The visitor stared at him.

'Ran off wi' that soldier boy, Mary Pask.'

Stupefied, the visitor did not reply. The old man lowered his gaze to the urn at his side.

'Brought her back, 'ave yer?'

Still, the visitor could not speak. He just stared and stared at the bags of the old man's jowls and his drooping custard face.

The Golden City

> The wind, the wind, the wind blows high,
> The rain is pouring from the sky ...

Maud stopped working and stared at the window. A distant stir of thunder added its faint growl to the chanting voices and the slap-slap-slap of the skipping rope.

> She is handsome, she is pretty,
> She's the flower of the Golden City.
> She is called by one, two, three.
> Pray who may her sweetheart be?

The Flower of the Golden City. How many years had passed since ...? Would the singing girls have believed that the words were as old as Maud herself? Or that she had once been handsome, been pretty?

Lightning flared and the dark sky spoke again, this time much closer. The girls abruptly ceased their singing. Maud listened to them running away, shrieking theatrically.

She continued to stare while the old song played hide-and-seek with her memory.

Charlie …

Charlie of the steel-flashing glance. The hidden, lustrous summer hours they had shared in Blunston's wood. Charlie, his sticks of black crayon, and his silhouette drawings of open-winged birds: the elegant, squat-faced gull; the goshawk's wide sweep; the heron, long of neck and beak.

Another crack of thunder and Maud was jolted back. She remembered where she was: it was her monthly stint of cleaning at the Institute. As she heard the first staccatos of rain lashing the roof, she gripped her mop purposefully, with both hands.

Then she fell motionless again, sunk in her memories.

Charlie …

He had gone to sea, some said, and became Commander of the Line. Others had heard he was a cattle farmer in Canada, as prosperous as the hills were high. He was a white chieftain on a Pacific island. He had fallen valiantly in South Africa, last man against the Boers. He was a rogue adventurer, living off charm, wits and a deck of cards. He was a painter man whose works hung in the aristocratic houses of London …

Maud knew only that she could never have kept him, her Charlie. For he was born to travel his own path.

So, when she was nineteen, she had married another. In their cramped home, her newborn was placed on the table in a linen basket. As the harsh, ravaging years passed, the basket was filled eleven times over.

Again, lightning raked the sky and a boom of thunder hauled Maud back to the present. The rain hammered the roof like an angry god. Maud remembered with a smile how

Charlie was a-feared of thunder. His eyes may have held the glint of threat, like the iron tips on his boots, which kicked sparks from the flagstones. But, come crash and roll and lightning, and Charlie would hide under the table.

She recalled the day she discovered his fear. The pictures unfolded in her mind one by one, each a frozen tableau. Charlie at the rabbit hole, bent, his steel eyes a-flash, shoulders set, holding the ferret box. The ferret tearing – whoosh! – into the hole, the scent in its nostrils and mad for the hunt. But too eager, too quick for Maud to hold the line. So fled and gone they were, ferret and grey rabbit together.

'Slipped through yer fingers!'

She faced Charlie's laughing taunt. But then the thunder struck. And, as they raced for the Institute garden shed, Charlie whimpering in fear, it was Maud's turn to laugh …

All the years, fled and gone. Charlie, her prowling, glint-eyed lover, fled and gone. Was no mark left behind, no print of the silver hours they had shared? No sign that they had breathed and laughed and burned?

Or was she just a foolish old woman, befuddled by shadows, echoes, shards, brittle voices and a wind that whispered the name of an old sweetheart? And which of her memories were but copies of memories, turned and twisted by the years?

And what if she and Charlie had not loved? What if they had never flared and spun and soared in a wooded summer? What would it matter?

Black silk, Charlie had called her hair. Well, an ancient bun of grey might have replaced her silk, and an old fool she may be now, and nothing of Charlie's breath and flesh remaining, or his mocking eyes, or her imprint on his heart. But they had loved! She knew, in the face of the indifferent world, that they had loved. For what else had she ever had?

As the rain flailed and blackened the windows of the Institute, she yearned for a sign, some confirmation that they had shared treasure before the coming of the poor, wasted years.

Another flash and a crack of thunder – and the mop clattered to her feet. Maud clutched her mouth. And remembered ...

The black torrent. Their race to the garden shed in the shaking thunder. Tools hanging on iron hooks: hoe, scythe, rake, delving spades. Charlie diving beneath the table, laughing to cover his fear, reaching ...

'Hold me, Maudie ...'

Maud laughing, mocking, then climbing under the table to join him, steel and silk. And there she held him, possessed him, in the thrusting storm and the thunder.

> The wind, the wind, the wind blows high,
> The rain is pouring from the sky ...

With her hand to her mouth, Maud hobbled to the Institute door, dragged it open. The torrent, rising to a frenzy, was carving jagged canyons in the gravel before her. So she could only slither her way forward, inch by inch. Another sickening crash of thunder and her scalp leapt.

The door of the garden shed was unlocked, as it had always been. She lurched inside and, peering into the gloom, made for the old table next to the wall. The wind swept the door wide open. Around her, the ancient tools banged and rattled on their hooks. In the half-light, she gripped the edge of the table, and lowered herself onto the dusty floor. Then she rolled painfully onto her side, facing the wall.

Immediately, a flash of lightning lit the open doorway, and gave her a glimpse of the flaking grey plaster before her eyes. As the answering thunder shook the roof, her blood raced. Then the lightning flared again, and again, and again. With each fleeting blaze, she caught another sight of the black-crayon silhouette on the wall.

Her heart full, Maud gazed in rapture at the shape of the soaring raven, and its fanned tail and the contours of its wide, jagged wings.

Epilogue

Jean: *All our older sisters left to go into service. 'Skivvying' some called it. I wasn't in service for long though. I got dismissed from every job I ever had, 'cos I was boy-crazy at the time. But Daisy and Hilda – the two oldest – they were travelling companions to well-off ladies. And once Doreen got hand-me-downs from the family sister Daisy worked for – posh dresses and knickers to match! She was lucky, but I was too old to get anything. Well, I didn't mind her getting the dress. It was the matching knickers that made me mad! But then, they wouldn't have been any good to hold my gooseberries in, would they?*

Doreen: *We had two schoolteachers. One was Mrs Savage. She was savage by name and nature, she really was. She loved to use that cane. Ooh, wasn't she cruel? But Miss Crowe, she was a nice-looking lady, curly-haired. A sports teacher. Coo, didn't she get us running around that field? She used the cane too, though I can honestly say I never got caned. I never opened my mouth, you see. I was a little goody-goody. But once, Miss Crowe, she gave Jean such a caning across the back that Mum came down to school next morning to sort her out. And, do you know, that Miss Crowe knitted mufflers for each of us, as a sort of apology?*

Joanie: *I used to pump the bellows behind the organ, where my friend Grace Cook played. You didn't have to keep to the rhythm. I wouldn't have been any good at that. You just had to keep it well pumped up so the organist could continue playing. Well, this was when we had soldiers stationed in the village. And, do you know, I had*

my eye on them soldiers in the congregation, so I tried to
show off. I made pretend I was singing – you know,
miming – and I forgot to keep me bellows pumped!

Molly: *The Nunns had nits in their hair – the nitty
Nunns, we called them. They had shaved heads, so we
knew. Their clothes were hand-me-downs, like every kid's,
but with buttons missing and torn clothing. And you
could see their toes in their lace-up boots. Everyone used to
say they were diseased. But Mum never forbade any of us
kids from playing with them. Well, the Nunns – the two
brothers – they came back to the village together much later.
Lovely chaps, in a lovely car. Smashing chaps, they were,
everybody said. They were asking around. It's nice to know
that they made good in the end, isn't it?*

Those Nunn brothers would have found the old village
transformed. In fact, it's something of an East Anglian
showpiece nowadays. Its old timberframe cottages have
been renovated and given fanciful rustic names: 'Keswick
End', 'Cookes Forge Barn', 'Ashdown Cottage'. The Six
Bells, where good ol' boys used to meet over their tankards,
is an upmarket tavern now. Patrons arrive for lunch in four-
wheel-drives and family estate wagons.

The low wall by the old post office is still there, where
boys and girls used to do their flirting. But it is crumbling
badly now, like the church moat where Jean had her first
covert smoke. There was talk in the Parish Council about
rebuilding it. But a good deal of collapsed earth would
have to be removed first, and a jetsam of tangled roots
unclogged, and the hedge replanted.

A cluster of smart new homes stands where the garage
used to sell accumulators for faded wireless sets. The old
allotments have been covered by housing too. The slate-
roofed schoolhouse is a residence now, its privacy guarded
by wooden hoarding. The Old Rectory, first home of the
Flower Show, is no more.

The Flower Show itself is still staged though, every summer. Retaining its character and name, it has never become a 'fete' or a 'festival'. As ever, prizes are awarded for beetroot and chrysanthemums and red onions. But there are also trophies for patio enhancement these days, and for scenic photography. During the afternoon, children stage a dance on the village green in baseball caps and Ghostbuster T-shirts, stalked by parents with phone cameras.

Set back from the main street, estates of semi-detacheds are occupied by 'bloody interlopers'. That's what the sisters' father used to call newcomers to the village – not that there were many in his day. Some of the current breed of interlopers have faces more dusky than Uncle Darkie's. And a large proportion of them are young families. They have brought enterprise and new blood to the village, and keep it attractive and alive.

The church tower has a pretty blue-faced clock now, and a weathervane on each corner. Scattered in the porch are leaflets – *Employers Liability Act* and *Domestic Violence and Abuse* – and handwritten notices – 'Missing from Hazel Drive area. Pure white male cat, one year old. Please call …'. The built-in collection box 'is emptied on a daily basis', so the Ecclesiastical Insurance Group tells us.

Outside, puckish weatherbeaten gargoyles stare at the cemetery, that silent barometer of continuity and change. The engraved memorials which the Reverend used to study on his early morning prowls – they are still there, of course: permanent reminders of men, women and – all too often – children who lived practically all their lives within the parish boundary, and were then laid in the sod of its ancient church.

It is the works of Victorian and Edwardian stonemasons that catch the eye. They lean and sag in spectacular varieties of shape, size and decay: green-mottled crucifixes, a grainy sarcophagus, crumbling vaults. Mould has taken its grip, and grey tendrils sprawl across granite slabs, pressed by the winds of the years. Many of the epitaphs are clogged by earth and moss, or have been effaced completely. The newer stones are of polished marble with bright lettering, yellow on black. At the base of some, pansies and violets stand in tiny vases and jam jars, among clumps of nettles.

The sisters' parents, Olli and Maud, are buried in the cemetery. Of this, the sisters are sure. But, to the regret of all of them, the graves are not marked, nor can they be traced.

The brooding church is the most enduring physical monument to the life the sisters knew. Strong was its influence on their girlhood. Molly, Doreen and Joanie were christened together at its ancient font, as babies of the village had been for more than 700 years. (Jean wasn't allowed to take part 'in case I started to make the others laugh.') They remember the event, all of them. Joanie was given *Jackanapes* and *Little Women* on the day, and Doreen feels sure she got *Little Women* too, and probably *The Water Babies*. Molly can't remember getting any books, but she knows that just family were there – 'not Dad, of course, he never went to church' – so the pews were as good as empty.

'I loved me hymns,' recalls Jean. 'The numbers of the hymns to be sung were hung up by the pulpit. I could connect all the numbers to the hymns. And they stayed connected in my memory for years afterwards.' True this may be. But, in point of fact, none of the sisters kept up their churchgoing in adulthood. Neither did they remain particularly God-fearing. Perhaps all that enforced churchgoing and Sunday schooling was more than enough for them.

They all have strong memories of the season when hundreds of lambs would be milling around the fields. 'We had to laugh,' says Jean, 'the newborn lambs would be so unsteady on their legs, staggering around like drunks. They'd try to get to their feet. You know, wobble, wobble, wobble. And there was the mother, shoving them with her nose, prodding them to make them get moving. It was so funny!'

But, truth to tell, the sisters seem to have taken little interest in the animals around them. There was Aunt Nelly's pig, and their Dad worked with horses for a while ('which we thought were a bit risky when they came right up to you,' says Jean). But considering they lived in a village, the sisters do not seem to have had that much contact with animals.

And none of them became very adept at naming the creatures of the fields, the rivers or the skies. For example, they all remember the spectacular massed flocks of birds on the woodshed before the autumn migration. But they cannot tell a house martin from a swift from a swallow. Evidently, nature's attractions lost out to other priorities: flirting with boys, steering clear of punishment, baiting their brother Jack – and getting more to eat.

Let me not imply that the sisters ever went hungry, for they insist that they did not. At the same time, food and mealtimes have a central place in their collective memory and they are always readier to discuss them than, say, livestock or wildlife.

Since everyone in the village grew vegetables on their property, few ever knew real hunger. Potatoes there were aplenty, and broad beans, cabbage, sprouts and onions. Mum and Dad also had a Victoria plum tree in the back garden, gooseberry and blackcurrant bushes, and three apple trees. Beetroot, rhubarb and celery were abundantly grown, and were good for you.

Joanie remembers with particular disgruntlement one washday when a lump of margarine was dumped on a plate of celery – 'and that was our dinner!' Boring and predictable such meals may have been, and lacking in variety. And some were unanimously detested: tapioca ('like snot'), swedes ('Mother would mix them with potatoes, so as to get them into us') and endless winter breakfasts of hot bread and milk.

But this food filled bellies and was nourishing. And – the key point – come dinner time, there was always a meal on the table. In this regard, Mother was typical of a generation of exhausted, heroic women who were engaged in the continual battle to feed their family and who grew old before their time.

There was a rhythm to the meals: the children knew what was coming, more or less. Sunday was special: roast with trimmings, Yorkshire pudding, baked potatoes. Sunday also brought prunes for tea or a slice of plain yellow cake, or broken biscuits bought cheap from the village shop.

That Sunday roast would have to last three days, for it would appear again, cold, on the Monday (washing day) and the remainder would get heated up with bits and pieces on Tuesday. The rotation called for suet dumplings and stew on Wednesday. Thursday brought suet pudding, drawn together (with meat and gravy) into a piece of cloth tied with string. The family would have that suet pudding twice: once with the cooked dish; later, as a sweet, with flour and golden syrup or jam. On Friday, the fish van came round the village. And come Saturday, the pot of stew would be on the table again.

A deep incision in the memory of all the sisters has been left by rabbit stew – in particular, the stench that accompanied the skinning, degutting and cleaning of the animal. Dad would usually buy the rabbit in the pub, from someone who had managed to poach a brace (a ritual alluded to in the 'Tutankhamen' story). Mother and children would then share the remaining work till the pot was brought to simmer over the open grate.

It is with some disbelief that the sisters remember that stewpot. 'It used to be permanently sooty on the outside,' Jean recalls, 'because it was just on an open fire, you know. It seemed to be boiling forever. How did it not burn up? And we always had that big sooty pot on the table for cooked meals, full of stew and dumplings and what-have-you. It came straight off the hob, and stood there on the dinner table with its sooty ring. You wouldn't credit it nowadays!'

As the years passed, the variety of diversions open to children became gradually richer. There was radio in the home now, and the year that Molly turned five brought the opening of the local Odeon cinema.

Public transport was entering villagers' lives. Soon there was no need, as Molly remembers, 'to walk to town with Mum with a pushchair to get the groceries, from Liptons or Home and Colonial.' And between the births of the oldest and youngest of the four sisters, the number of motor cars tripled. Jean remembers the first one in the village, standing outside the Rectory. ('I loved warming my hands on the grill at the front.') And, by the time they were of secondary school age, all of the girls had to travel on the school bus.

During or after the war – 'Our War', in their terminology, in contrast to 'Dad's War' – all four left the village and married servicemen in uniform. Despite nostalgic affection for the world of their childhood, they agree that the new one they entered was far better. It was noisier, and faster, and its horizons were unimaginably wider. For the sisters, doors were opened such as no earlier generation had ever known. And they put the village behind them, for good.

Oh, and one more – very intriguing – thing. I had expected that, in a rural community between the wars, everyone would know each other's business. The sisters' reminiscences reveal that this was not so. Despite the spying endeavours of the pinnie ladies and their like, there were homes whose occupants were practically unknown – 'mystery people' who were never seen at church and lived in secluded anonymity.

In the corner of the cemetery, two parallel graves each bear the German inscription *Ruhe in Frieden*: 'Rest in Peace'. Born 33 years apart, Martha and Margot (maiden name: Beyer) were evidently mother and daughter. Margot was married to one 'Edward (Vic) Oliver MBE', who rests alongside them. The signs are that, before being buried in the village, this trio lived there for roughly the same span of years as Jean, Doreen, Joan and Molly did.

But not one of the sisters can remember Martha or Margot or Edward.

Is there a tale here, of horizons far from English shores, of trains and ships, furtive escapes and packed bundles, of risk and anxiety, hopes, heartbreak and flight? Was native German spoken in the village? Perhaps in low, curbed voices, in the muddled years of the Thirties, and during the war which followed? Did Martha and Margot live out their lives as fugitives within the prison of their Suffolk village? For, as we have seen, it is entirely feasible that three people could have lived in total retreat, beneath the same roof, and known to no one.

Martha and Margot, née Beyer, *Ruhe in Frieden.*

A tale begs to be told ...

Postscript

The grand events that moved the world could shake hearts and minds in the village too. But, just as likely, such events would pass unnoticed. Here, for the sake of historical focus, are some of those which marked the years of the sisters' childhood.

In 1924, the year that Jean was born ...

Britain acquired its first Labour Government, under Ramsey MacDonald.

A national air transport company – Imperial Airways – was launched.

The deaths were announced of British climbers Mallory and Irvine, on the last stage of an attempt to reach the summit of Mount Everest.

Lenin died and Stalin began his purges to clear the path for his leadership of the Soviet Union.

In 1926, the year of Doreen's birth ...

The Midwives and Maternity Homes Act tightened the regulations against unqualified midwives.

Franco became General of Spain.

In Britain, conflict between the coalminers and the government led to a general strike.

The Memorial Theatre at Stratford-upon-Avon was destroyed by fire. An appeal fund for its rebuilding was launched by signatories including Stanley Baldwin, Ramsey MacDonald and Thomas Hardy.

The sudden death of film star Rudolph Valentino caused mass grief and hysteria around the world.

In 1929, Joanie's year of birth ...

The King, on his return from illness, received a tumultuous welcome by crowds along a two-and-a-half-mile route through the West End.

The first latex condoms appeared in Britain.

Miss Margaret Bondfield was appointed Minister of Labour, the first woman to serve in a British cabinet.

The first sound newsreels for cinema were produced in Britain.

Rhodes scholarships to Germany were resumed for the first time since the Great War.

The Boy Scouts World Jamboree at Arrowe Park, Birkenhead, drew 50,000 participants from more than forty countries.

In 1930, when the oldest sister, Jean, turned six ...

Cricketer Don Bradman, 21, scored a world record 452 not out for New South Wales against Queensland.

Mahatma Gandhi's campaign for Indian independence began at Ahmedabad and proceeded to a campaign of civil disobedience against the salt-manufacturing laws.

The 'Poor Law' became 'Public Assistance' and the work of the Guardians of the Poor was transferred to county borough councils and county councils.

The British Gliding Association, devoted to 'flight in motorless aeroplanes', awarded its first certificates for proficiency.

Sir Henry Segrave met his death on Lake Windermere after setting a new world speed record on water: 103mph.

John Masefield, former sailor, bartender and beachcomber, was appointed as the 18th Poet Laureate, following the death of Robert Bridges.

The R101 airship crashed in Beauvais, France, killing forty six.

In 1931, when Jean turned seven, Doreen four and Joanie three ...

6.1% of the occupied workforce were in agriculture.

Professor Albert Einstein gave his third and last lecture on the theory of relativity at Rhodes House.

The Committee on National Expenditure reported that £120 million had to be gained by fresh taxation or by economy in order to achieve a balanced budget by 1932.

The Labour government resigned. His Majesty asked Ramsey MacDonald to form a national government, to meet the financial emergency.

The Bank of England came off the Gold Standard and appeals were made to the population not to engage in hoarding.

Cunard Steamship Company suspended shipbuilding at Clydeside.

Captain Malcolm Campbell set a new land speed record – 246mph – in Blue Bird before 30,000 spectators on Daytona Beach, Florida.

Senior Liberal peer Lord Beauchamp fled Britain when it appeared likely that his homosexuality was about to be exposed.

In 1932, when the youngest sister, Molly, was born ...

The first airmail service to Cape Town began: 20,000 letters and 150 parcels were transported from Croydon in a four-engined Helena airliner.

The Board of Control of Ballroom Dancing decided that the slow foxtrot and the quickstep were to be danced from four to six bars to the minute slower.

Author Edgar Wallace died, aged 56.

The Lausanne Conference on reparations and war debts took place in the shadow of the world economic crisis.

Eighty-four Dartmoor convicts were shot or injured, following a mutiny of 400 prisoners.

King George V became the first British monarch to make a Christmas broadcast.

In 1933, when Jean had her ninth birthday, and the youngest, Molly, her first ...

The *Daily Express* became the largest-selling daily, overtaking the *Daily Mail.*

1,196,000 private motor vehicles were in use.

Adolf Hitler became Chancellor of Germany.

John Galsworthy died, aged 65.

Mahatma Gandhi was sentenced to prison in India.

Following an independent investigation and after interviewing fifty-one eye witnesses, Lieutenant Commander R.T. Gould, R.N., reported: 'There can, at all events, be little question that Loch Ness contains at least one specimen of the rarest and least-known of all living creatures.'

In the next year, 1934, when the oldest sister, Jean, turned 10 ...

The Road Traffic Act introduced a 30mph speed limit in built-up areas and a compulsory driving test.

King Leopold of the Belgians was killed by a fall while rock-climbing near Namur.

A fashion magazine reported that 'in London, women are wearing check silk blouses with bibs and bows of the same material, loudish check skirts and plain cardigan coats and innumerable tones of Chinese jade-blue or green for sports woollies, house dresses or swagger suits'.

7,273 deaths on the roads were reported. 231,698 were injured.

Waterloo Bridge was demolished.

Field Marshal von Hindenburg died and King Alexander of Yugoslavia was assassinated.

The Queen Mary – 'the greatest ship in the world' – was launched at Clydebank.

261 died in a mining disaster at Gresford.

In 1935, when Jean was eleven, Doreen nine, Joanie six and Molly three ...

'We are the Ovaltinies, little girls and boys' was broadcast for the first time.

The London Borough of Lambeth put up Belisha beacons made of compressed steel, to prevent vandalism and theft.

For the Royal Jubilee celebrations, the Houses of Parliament and the entire fleet at the Spithead naval review were floodlit.

In the United States, Bruno Hauptmann was found guilty of the murder of the Lindbergh baby.

Jack Hobbs, master batsman, retired, after scoring 197 first-class centuries.

Sir Malcolm Campbell, driving Blue Bird at Daytona Beach, set a new land speed record of 276mph.

And the Postmaster General declared that 'the day has now come – or will come this year – when, in addition to listening at a turn of the switch to music and speech, it will be possible for many to see as well as hear from their firesides what is happening at some distant point.'